# KINDRED SPIRITS

*Books by Marilyn Meredith*

Calling the Dead
Judgment Fire
Deadly Omen
Unequally Yoked
Wing Beat
Intervention
Kindred Spirits

# MARILYN MEREDITH

# KINDRED SPIRITS

## TEMPE CRABTREE
### MYSTERY SERIES

Mundania Press

Cincinnati, Ohio

A Mundania Press Production
Mundania Press LLC
6470A Glenway Avenue, #109
Cincinnati, Ohio 45211-5222

To order additional copies of this book, contact:
books@mundania.com
www.mundania.com

Cover Art © 2008 by Anna Winsom
Edited by Jade Falconer
Book Design by Daniel J. Reitz, Sr.
Production by Bob Sanders
Marketing and Promotion by Skyla Dawn Cameron

Trade Paperback ISBN: 978-1-59426-735-2
eBook ISBN: 978-1-59426-734-5

First Edition • August 2008

Mundania Press LLC
Printed in the United States of America
10   9   8   7   6   5   4   3   2   1

# DEDICATED TO

To the Tolowa people—true survivors.

And most importantly, to Junie Mahoney, a remarkable woman who in real life told me some of the history, legends and stories about her people.

To my good friend and writing mentor of many, many years, Willma Gore, who kindly did the first edit of the manuscript.

This is a work of fiction. Some of the things depicted may not be correct—but were needed to work for the story. My apologies to the Del Norte County Sheriff's deputies who are not portrayed in a favorable manner—again this was needed for the story.

"The reservations were founded on the principle, not of attempting to do something for the native, but getting him out of the white man's way as cheaply and hurriedly as possible."
—Alfred Kroeber, Anthropologist


"Reservations became a convenient place to dump the natives when whites ran out of bullets or the nerve to murder."
—Anonymous, late 20$^{th}$ century

Indians were denied access to critical food and medicine by fences and fictional property "rights" of the whites. Where the native people fished became clogged by mining and logging debris. Animals that they hunted for food were slaughtered or driven from their usual habitats. Native plants died because irrigation lowered the water tables. Swamps, that had once been resources for food and game, were drained from farm land. Farm animals ate the grasses, seeds and nuts that were food for the natives.

Indian people starved to death by the hundreds.

# CHAPTER 1

Before Deputy Tempe Crabtree saw the evidence of the forest fire, she could smell it. Smoke was heavy in the air and got thicker as she drove up the highway into the mountains. Monday was one of her days off, but when something happened in her jurisdiction she was often the first responder. Her instructions from the sheriff's sub-station in Dennison were to make sure everyone who lived in the path of the fire, which started in the higher elevations of Bear Creek canyon, had obeyed evacuation orders.

As resident deputy of the large but sparsely populated area around the mountain community of Bear Creek, Tempe's job usually consisted of making traffic stops, arresting drunk drivers, solving problems among neighbors, and looking for lost children or cattle. Along with the highway patrol, Tempe was the law in the community, located in the southern Sierra where the foothills grew into mountains.

The last estimate Tempe had heard about the fast moving fire was it covered more than 1100 acres. She was stopped at the staging area by a highway patrolman. She knew him by sight though she couldn't remember his name.

Though his uniform still had sharp creases, large circles of dampness crept from his underarms. Opaque sunglasses covered his eyes. He put both hands on the open window of her Blazer as he bent down to speak to her. "Where're you headed, Deputy?"

"My orders are to check out some of the houses in the

path of the fire. Make sure everyone's out."

"Be careful you don't put yourself in danger. It's one fast-moving fire. It's in a rough area where they haven't been able to get any personnel in yet. They're doing lots of water drops. All the roads are closed from here on up."

"Thanks for the warning. I know some of the folks who may not have received the word yet."

Tempe drove by a private airstrip that had been taken over as the fire command post. Men and equipment, fire engines, water tenders and bulldozers were dispatched from there, as well as truckloads of hand crews.

Leaving her window down, Tempe drove around the traffic cones that blocked the road. She planned to stop first at the Donaldsons', but when she reached their place they were loading horses into a trailer, obviously on their way out.

The higher she drove on the winding road, the darker the sky, the thicker the smoke, and the harder it was to breathe. Gray ash showered her white Blazer. She passed fire trucks and men heading upward to fight the fire. In her heart she was thankful her son, Blair, was already back on the coast for his last year in college or he'd be on the fire lines. Fighting fire had been his first love since the age of sixteen when he began hanging around Bear Creek's fire station.

Tempe stopped at several homes hidden down winding trails or perched on hilltops, surrounded by pine, cedar trees and underbrush. Most homes were deserted, with signs of hurried evacuation.

Loaded pick-up trucks drove down the hill, some pulling horse or cattle trailers, not getting out any too soon from the looks of the black sky and the large amount of raining ash.

She had one more place to check. A beautiful home and separate studio built of sugar pine stood atop a knoll surrounded by chaparral, and a thick pine forest. Tempe had been there once on a domestic abuse call. The owner, a well-known artist, Vanessa Ainsworth, now lived alone since her boyfriend had been served a restraining order. If Vanessa wasn't gone already, Tempe hoped to help her collect her animals and paintings and carry some of them out for her.

When Tempe made the last turn before Vanessa's she halted at a horrifying sight.

# CHAPTER TWO

A fire truck and water tender blocked her way. Firefighters in their black and yellow-striped turnout coats held hoses,the spray aimed at a huge wall of flames moving down the hillside toward the road.

"Oh, dear God," Tempe groaned. She braked and climbed out of the Blazer. Once she reached the fireman who seemed to be directing the operation, she yelled over the roar of the fire. "Do you know if Vanessa Ainsworth got out all right?"

His voice hoarse, the firefighter answered, "Hopefully everyone evacuated. The fire was moving too fast for us to go any higher. We're expecting some water drops anytime now."

"Thanks and good luck." Absently tucking stray strands of her nearly black hair into the long braid that hung down her back, Tempe climbed into the Blazer and headed towards town. There was nothing more for her to do here.

The road was crowded with evacuees driving toward town, and fire equipment moving toward the fire, slowing travel both ways. When she came to the A-frame building that housed the community church that her husband, Hutch, pastored, she was surprised to see that many of the trucks, fifth-wheels, travel trailers and one motor home had stopped in the parking lot. Hutch was talking animatedly to the owner of the pack station who was unloading horses from a large trailer.

Tempe pulled in and parked. Hutch hurried toward her. Sliding from the Blazer, she asked, "What's going on?"

"The church is serving as an emergency shelter for those who have nowhere else to go. The women from church are preparing sandwiches and drinks." He chuckled. "Some folks don't have any trouble sleeping on the pews during the sermon so maybe they can serve as temporary beds."

Scanning the nearly full parking lot, Tempe asked, "You haven't seen Vanessa Ainsworth, have you?"

Hutch ran his fingers through his already disheveled auburn hair. "She's the artist, isn't she? Not sure I'd recognize her if I did see her."

"I'll walk around and see who's here."

"Good idea. I have to make a list of supplies we'll need. Toilet paper for sure. We're not equipped for the number of people who may be using our facilities. Harry Plover is making a run to Dennison for me." Hutch trotted toward the church.

He hadn't kissed her. Unusual, but things had been strained between them the last two years, another reason she was glad Blair was away at college and busy with his friends who shared his interest in fire-fighting.

It all began with the building of the Bear Mountain Indian Casino on the Bear Creek Reservation. When the casino was in the planning stages, Hutch, along with several other area ministers and their parishioners staged a protest, complete with signs. They marched along the main highway near the road that led to the reservation. It was an embarrassment to Tempe who was part Native American. Many of her Indian friends had commented on her husband's actions.

Hutch's argument to Tempe was always the same. "Gambling is evil and it will lead to further evils."

Tempe had countered with, "But the casino will breathe life back into the reservation. It will provide jobs for the Indians where they live."

Once the casino became a reality, both were proved right. Yes, there were some people who became addicted to gambling, a few senior citizens who lost their social security money as soon as they cashed their checks, and those who foolishly gambled away their monthly house payments or rent money.

On the brighter side, the casino's profits enabled the native people to build and staff a new health center on the reservation and a pre-school. New homes were built and more businesses created. The unemployment rate on the rez dropped from 80% to 25%. More businesses were developed on and off the reservation so that tribal members would have choices about employment besides the casino.

Tempe knew that the pluses from the casino far outweighed any of the minuses connected with gambling. No drinking was allowed on casino grounds, so that wasn't something Hutch could add to his complaints.

For a while they were unable to have a conversation on this subject without an argument. Now that the casino had been a fact for nearly two years, it seldom came up in conversation. Perhaps that was because they didn't have many conversations anymore except on a superficial level.

Tempe circled the parking lot. The Benders, an older retired couple whose property was a couple of miles down from Vanessa's place, had set up camp beside their travel trailer. Settled in folding chairs, their golden retriever resting by their feet, they smiled when Tempe approached.

After greeting one another, Tempe asked, "Have you seen Vanessa Ainsworth? I'm wondering if she made it down from her place."

Mr. Bender, knobby knees protruding from khaki shorts, shook his balding head, where what was left of his gray hair stuck up in tufts. "Haven't seen her."

His wife, a dark smudge of ash on her wrinkled cheek said, "I tried calling her before we left but didn't get an answer. I supposed she was out of town at one of her art shows."

"I certainly hope so." Tempe made her way around the parking lot, speaking to each person and asking about Vanessa. Unfortunately, though many knew about the artist and what she looked like, few had made her acquaintance and no one had seen her recently.

After completing her rounds, Tempe entered the church.

She could hear Hutch's voice coming from his office. Sunshine streamed though the stained glass window at the front of the sanctuary and splashed a rainbow of colors over the rows of oak pews. A sense of serenity contrasted with the cartons of bottled water stacked against the cedar paneled walls, and sleeping bags tossed in a pile.

Tempe stood in the open doorway of the small church office. Hutch held the phone to his ear with his shoulder, his fingers grasping a pen poised above a notepad already filled with writing. He smiled and waved her inside. Hutch wasn't merely a preacher, but a minister to his flock and community in the true sense of his profession. Using church funds specified for benevolence, and sometimes his own, Hutch often paid electric bills for persons down on their luck, and first and last month's rent for a homeless family. He counseled couples in trouble, prayed with and for the sick and the dying at home or in the hospital. He received almost as many emergency telephone calls in the middle of the night as his deputy wife.

He hung up the phone and asked, "Any luck finding the missing artist?"

"She's not here. I'm hoping she wasn't home when the fire neared her house. Even if she wasn't there, any animals she has are still in danger."

He frowned and shook his head. "Any news about the fire?"

"It's still threatening houses in the upper mountains. I drove up as far as I could go. The fire is raging. I don't think there's any containment yet."

"This is certainly a bad one." Hutch scanned his notes, his hand hovering over the phone.

Tempe could tell he was thinking about what he needed to do next. "You're busy. I'll head down to town and ask around to learn if anyone has seen or heard from Vanessa."

❧❧

Most of those Tempe ran into at the market or on the street had no idea who Vanessa was or, if they did, hadn't seen her. The fact that the woman was consumed by the pursuit of her talent hadn't left time to make many friends. Tempe wondered how she'd managed to connect with her ex-boyfriend, Eric Figueroa. After he'd moved out of Vanessa's home, he'd rented a small trailer in the park near the river.

Like the weather-worn "Bear Creek Trailer Park" sign, the area had seen better days. The terraced sites were only big enough for single-wide mobile homes. Some spaces held travel trailers or fifth wheels. It was one of the few low-rent spots left in Bear Creek. Eric's home was battered and badly in need of paint, contrasting sharply with his nearly new, bright red Jeep parked nearby. Squashed beer cans decorated the wooden steps leading to the screen door, and the front door gaped open.

Peering into the dim interior, Tempe knocked and called out, "Eric Figueroa. It's Deputy Crabtree. I need to talk to you."

A sleepy-eyed, bare-chested man appeared. Dark blue satin running shorts hung on narrow hips. Handsome, a dark Latin-lover type with long-lashed soulful eyes, Eric seemed young and not the type the reclusive Vanessa would have fallen for. But what did Tempe know? She'd only had two men in her life. Her first husband, Blair's father, who died in the line of duty as a highway patrolman, and now Hutch.

"Yeah? What do you want?" Eric growled as he ran his hand over the top of his short black hair. A day's growth of beard shadowed his olive skin.

"I wondered if you'd heard or seen anything of Vanessa today."

Eric remained on the other side of the screen door. "She has a restraining order against me, remember?"

"Yes, I know, but I'm concerned about her safety. The fire is burning near her house. I was unable to get up there. I was hoping you might have heard from her."

While Tempe spoke, Eric's dark eyebrows nearly met as a frown creased his forehead. "Do you know if she was home?"

"That's what I was hoping to find out from you."

He opened the screen door and stepped out on the porch beside her. He was barefooted and the same height as Tempe's five foot eight. "I better see if I can get through."

"Even if there wasn't a restraining order against you contacting her, you couldn't get up there. The road is closed to all civilians, even homeowners. I was hoping you'd heard from her, or perhaps know where she might have gone to wait out the fire."

For a moment, Eric stared down at the trailer below his. When he turned back to face Tempe, he threw his arms out to his sides. "There's no one. Vanessa doesn't have close friends. When she's painting, she doesn't sleep or eat. When I was with her, I took lunch out to the studio. In the evening I begged her to come in for supper. I fixed that too. Believe it or not, that's what all our arguments were about. Me making her a delicious dinner, her not coming in until the food was cold. When she was working on a new project, she couldn't focus on anything else—even eating. Nothing could interrupt her— not even a forest fire." He blinked and his lower lip quivered. "Oh, my God, do you suppose...?"

His concern seemed genuine, but Tempe remembered the rage in his eyes and how his olive complexion had turned purple when she'd arrived at the sugar pine chateau in answer to Vanessa's 9-1-1 call.

"I want him out of here...now!" Vanessa had said, her hands on hips. Her short-cropped graying hair mussed, a paint-smeared, oversized shirt camouflaging what Tempe knew was a trim figure. Colorful paint splotches decorated Vanessa's jeans.

"What's the problem?" Tempe asked.

Vanessa glared at Eric. "I won't be threatened by a guest in my home. Pack up your things and leave."

"Fine. I'll be out of here in ten minutes." Eric stomped up the circular stairs to what looked like a loft.

"Did he hurt you?" Tempe asked.

"Not yet, but I know the signs. My ex-husband was controlling and mentally abusive before he hit me the first and last time. I'm not going through that again."

"If Eric hasn't done anything physical, I won't be able to

arrest him, but I will escort him down the mountain. You can always go into Dennison tomorrow and get a restraining order."

"I know what to do." Vanessa crossed her arms over her bosom. She glared at Eric as he clattered down the stairs carrying a large duffel bag in one hand, guitar case in the other.

"You're going to miss me when you get hungry," Eric said.

"Just leave and don't come back," Vanessa threw after him, her voice shrill. To Tempe, she added, "Please make sure he actually leaves."

At that time Tempe hadn't considered Eric an actual threat to Vanessa. It may have been the artist's way to end a relationship she no longer wanted.

Observing Eric's expressed concern for Vanessa's safety now, Tempe wondered about him. "In case I need to talk to you again, where can I find you?"

"When I'm not here, I'm working."

"Where is that?"

"I tend bar at Feldman's Sports Bar and Grill." He glanced at his watch. "I go on duty at six."

Feldman's was a fairly new and quite popular hang-out located near Lake Dennison. It was frequented by the younger set.

"Thanks for being cooperative," Tempe said.

Eric touched her arm. "If you find anything out about Vanessa, will you let me know?"

❧❧

Tempe's next stop was the fire station. The bays were open and empty, the two engines occupied by the forest fire. One volunteer manned the phone; Jack Malone, a retired electrician. A tan uniform shirt barely covered the substantial belly that hung over his belted jeans.

"Hey, Deputy Crabtree." A grin spread over Jack's broad, sun-tanned face. "What can I do for you?"

"I wonder if you have news about the fire."

"So far it's only about five percent contained. It's moving

in a north-easterly direction. They're guessing it was caused by human hand. We've got about 800 fire fighters and support personnel working the incident. The firefighters, aided by water-dropping helicopters, are battling high temperatures and steep terrains." He sounded like a newscaster reading from a teleprompter.

Finally, Tempe interrupted. "Have there been any reports of injuries or fatalities?"

Jack brushed his sandy gray buzz cut with his hand. "We've had three minor injuries that were taken care of at the base camp. That's all I know about."

❧❧

Tempe came home to an empty house for her dinner. She fixed a fried egg sandwich and ate alone. Hutch was probably still at the church helping the evacuees. She watched the news on TV. The Bear Creek fire was the headline story. The fire was moving toward groves of Giant Sequoia trees and the California Department of Forestry and the U.S. Forest Service were reported to be making a stand to protect the groves.

The phone rang as Tempe took the last bite of her food. Still chewing, she answered, "Deputy Crabtree."

Though he didn't identify himself, Tempe recognized Bear Creek's Fire Chief's voice, Pete Roundtree. "Tempe, you better get up here. We've found a body in the remains of a burned-out structure."

"Did you report it to the sheriff's department?" Tempe asked.

"Of course, but I thought you ought to take a look too."

"Do you know who it is?"

"We're waiting for the coroner and the detectives to get here so we haven't touched the body, but I suspect it's that artist lady, Vanessa Ainsworth."

# CHAPTER THREE

Tempe arrived on the scene about a half hour before the detectives and the coroner. When she slid out of the Blazer, she was immediately assaulted by the odor from the lingering smoke of the smoldering vegetation, burned buildings and the sickening stench of cooked flesh. Because it was late summer, it was still light enough to see. The sugar pine chalet had only been scorched by the fire, but the studio, which stood about forty feet from the main structure, was destroyed.

Pete met Tempe when she started up the hill. He was a good friend and fellow Yanduchi. His ancestry was apparent in his round face, black hair and chestnut coloring. He wore his helmet and turn-out coat and trousers. "We found the remains in what's left of the smaller building. There's something else I want you to see." Pete led the way across the ash-covered ground.

Tempe barely recognized the place from when she'd last been there. Vanessa had told Tempe that she wanted her home to be surrounded by native plants. Unfortunately, that meant chaparral and other highly combustible growth. The homeowners who cleared away at least thirty or forty feet of vegetation, or even the hundred feet now mandated, had houses still intact..

Pete pointed out a spot near what had once been the front door of the studio—a charred lump with tufts of fur that Tempe guessed was Vanessa's German Shepherd. "Her dog. I'm surprised he didn't try to get away from the fire."

"He was trying to alert his mistress to the danger," Pete said. "Loyalty. She's still inside there." He gestured toward the burnt-out ruins.

Tempe glanced around and remembered the roar of the fire and the thick smoke. It seemed strange that Vanessa hadn't noticed, no matter how engrossed she was, and attempted an escape. "So sad. You better not show me anything else. The detectives won't be pleased to learn I've been walking around here."

"It's not a crime scene," Pete said.

"They'll want it treated it like one until they know for sure." Tempe made her way back down the hill. She'd left her Blazer behind Pete's fire engine. A water tender was farther up the road.

Detectives Morrison and Richards arrived in their black Mercury SUV, a huge step up from the old, battered Plymouth they used to drive.

Richards squinted at Tempe as he slid his angular frame out of the driver's seat.

The size of a line-backer, Morrison, his lumpy, round face in a perpetual frown, said, "I suppose you've already been messing around up there." His statement was directed as much at Tempe as Pete, but Pete answered.

"Haven't touched the body. Doesn't look like there was any foul play. Poor woman and her dog were trapped by the fast-moving fire." Pete pointed up the hill toward what remained of the studio.

Richards glanced around. "Too bad she didn't stay in the house. It doesn't look bad." Though the chateau still stood, the windows had been shattered.

Pete shook his head. "No, even if she'd been inside, I doubt she'd have lived through the intense heat and smoke."

"Hang around, Crabtree," Richards said. "We may need you to answer some questions."

The coroner arrived in his gray van with the county seal on the side. A portly man with a bald head, he huffed and puffed as he waddled up the hill. Tempe expected it wouldn't be long before they transported Vanessa's charred remains to the morgue.

Instead, Richards trotted down the hill, kicking up plumes of gray ash. "Crabtree," he hollered. "Get on your radio and get the crime scene investigator up here. We've got ourselves a murder victim."

Tempe knew better than to ask questions. She immediately used the radio in the Blazer to relay the information. Cell phones did not work in the high country; too many mountains blocked signals.

Richards and Morrison, along with the coroner, impatiently waited for the crime scene investigator. In the past, in the boonies Richards and Morrison had done their own investigating. Because of complaints from victims' families, especially those who watched TV crime shows, it was now routine to call the coroner and the crime scene investigator.

It was getting darker, The sun had disappeared, though the sky still glowed crimson from the fire. The coroner had found a tree stump to sit on.

Tempe leaned against the Blazer and watched the detectives. While waiting, they examined the dead dog. Morrison squatted beside it, poking the remains with a stick. He leapt to his feet and backed off. Richards leaned over and stared at whatever Morrison had discovered. Both of the men moved away and called the coroner over. Despite the gloom, Tempe could see that whatever had surprised the detectives, piqued the rotund coroner's interest too.

Her usual task would have been to keep the curious away. The road was closed to residents and the firefighters were much too busy to bother with what was going on. The detectives and the coroner bustled about, taking pictures, bending over objects, but they didn't enter the blackened skeleton of the studio. The detectives set up some portable lights which created eerie shadows.

It was nearly dark by the time the crime scene investigator arrived in a Ford van with the county seal on it, which she parked behind Tempe's Blazer. Andrea Crandall was around

Tempe's age, mid to late thirties. Tiny, with short blond hair, wearing a gray pantsuit with a plain black blouse, Dr. Crandall strode toward Tempe with her hand outstretched, her black equipment case in her other hand.

"What do we have here?"

"I don't know the details, only that someone was caught in the fire when it went through. The woman who owns the property hasn't been accounted for. Her dog is dead too."

Dr. Crandall pushed her tiny round glasses onto her head. She made a face in the direction of the men working on the hill. "Fools still don't have brains enough to use you, I suppose."

"I'm used to it," Tempe said.

Tempe knew from a prior conversation with Dr. Crandall, that though she certainly didn't look it, she was a quarter Native American. Several times she'd commiserated with Tempe about the way some of the men in the sheriff's department treated female deputies and even Dr. Crandall, despite her profession and credentials. She'd graduated with a master's degree in Criminology, and had her doctorate in Crime Scene Investigation. Gaining experience for several years in Ventura County, she then returned to her home town of Visalia and was appointed as the Crime Scene Investigator. No one but Tempe knew Dr. Crandall was part Indian, so the doctor didn't have to put up with the added prejudice.

Dr. Crandall grinned. "Those two aren't the least bit happy they have to wait for me before they can do much. Has the coroner taken a look at the body yet?"

"I'm not sure. It's pretty hard to see what they're doing up there. Firefighters discovered the body and told Pete Roundtree, the fire captain for Bear Creek. He's the one who called me. I suspect the firefighters tramped all over the scene. After all, they had a job to do."

Dr. Crandall nodded, absently fluffed her cropped curls, and headed up the hill.

Tempe watched as Dr. Crandall greeted the detectives and the coroner. She followed the coroner as he waddled in the direction of what was left of the studio and the charred remains of the victim. The doctor and the coroner leaned down and spent several minutes studying the corpse. Dr. Crawford opened her black box. Despite the temporary lights, Tempe was too far away to see what was happening.

Dr. Crandall rose and stepped over to the burned body of the dog. She called the detectives over and everyone knelt again. The coroner waved his arms to his assistant who, like Tempe, had been waiting by the coroner's van. Much younger and more physically fit than the coroner, the assistant pushed a gurney loaded with a large equipment box up the hill to the skeletal remains of the studio. It wasn't long before two plastic wrapped bundles atop the gurney were rolled down the hill and deposited in the coroner's vehicle.

"We've got a job for you, Crabtree," Richards hollered. "How about putting crime scene tape up to keep anyone from stomping around in the area while we're gone." It was an order, not a question. It was a good idea since firefighters might be coming through to check on hot spots.

While Tempe strung the tape she hoped they might let her in on what they'd learned, but it didn't happen.

The detectives dismantled the temporary lighting, throwing the scene into complete darkness except for the glow from the receding fire. Dr. Crandall came down the hill, followed by the detectives carrying their lighting equipment. Tempe trailed along behind. Morrison didn't even glance in Tempe's direction before climbing into the passenger side of their SUV.

Richards paused beside Tempe long enough to say, "You can go back to your regular duty now. We may be calling you for some more information tomorrow."

Before she could ask what kind of information, he jumped into the vehicle, started it and turned around.

Shaking her head, Dr. Crandall approached Tempe. Soot was on one cheek, another smudge on her forehead, and several dark splotches on the jacket of her suit and the knees of her pants. "Nice guys. Couldn't be bothered with bringing you up-to-date after making you hang around all evening."

"I'm used to it."

Smiling, Dr. Crandall said, "This is what we've got so far. Both our victim and the dog were shot. Probably happened long before the fire reached them."

Tempe nodded. "It had to be before they blocked off the road. After that, they didn't even allow residents, or even me, to come up here."

"We'll know a bit more after the autopsy, but not a whole lot. There's not much left of either corpse. We'll have to use dental records to make positive identification of the human remains, but it's a pretty safe assumption that the victim is the owner of the property."

"Vanessa Ainsworth." Tempe's heart sank even though she'd known that ever since she heard about the body found in the studio.

"I'll be back up here tomorrow to see if I can spot anything in the daylight that we overlooked tonight," Dr. Crandall said.

"Will you need me? Tomorrow is my day off." Tempe laughed. "Today was supposed to be too."

Dr. Crandall smiled. "Sounds like me. I'm called out anytime, day or night. Usually when I'm doing something special that I've planned for weeks. I'd better get going, and no, I won't need you but thanks for the offer."

❧❧

Hutch returned home from the church about the time Tempe's shift was over, but only to shower and change clothes. He gave Tempe a quick kiss and hurried off. The fire crisis would have to settle down in Bear Creek before Tempe and Hutch would have time to work on their relationship. And work was definitely needed. They certainly couldn't go on forever like they were now. Troubled, she went to bed.

# CHAPTER FOUR

In the morning when Tempe put a load of wash in the machine, Sergeant Guthrie called from the sheriff's substation in Dennison.

"Crabtree, Detectives Morrison and Richards would like to meet with you this morning. Get down here around ten." He hung up before she could remind him it was her day off.

From TV news, she learned the fire was estimated to be twenty-five percent contained and evacuations remained in effect. As long as the church was needed for a shelter, Hutch would be occupied. The fire seemed to be keeping everyone in Bear Creek busy; she hadn't had a single call last night. The much publicized road closure kept away the curious. No new crimes were reported, making the lives of Tempe and the deputies easier.

At half past nine, Tempe, in her khaki uniform, long black braid fastened with a silver barrette, was in her Blazer headed toward Dennison. Once she got out of the mountains, in her rearview mirror she could see the huge plume of smoke rising skyward. She drove past Dennison Lake and the many homes and orange groves that lined the highway as it widened to four lanes near the city. She made the turn that led to the substation, an unattractive, one story block building.

Though she was five minutes early, Richards and Morrison, wearing their usual attire of sport jackets, T-shirts and jeans, greeted her without smiles.

Sergeant Guthrie was a bit more pleasant. Rising slightly

from behind his desk, he grinned. "Glad you could make it, Crabtree. Take a seat." He pointed to a metal folding chair.

The office was tiny, barely enough room for the furniture crammed into the small space. With three big men occupying the other chairs, it felt claustrophobic.

Tempe nodded and sat, wondering what her required presence meant. She hadn't disobeyed anyone's orders, so she didn't expect a reprimand.

"Detectives Richards and Morrison have a request for you. You are under no obligation to accept. If you do, the department will make arrangements for a replacement for you in Bear Creek for the time you're gone. And there will be extra compensation for your time," Sergeant Guthrie said.

What on earth was this all about? Tempe shifted in her seat to face the detectives. As usual, Morrison, who sat next to her, glowered. His battered face showed no emotion.

Richards squinted even more than usual as he spoke. "We've done a background check on the murder victim."

Tempe frowned. "Excuse me, who are you referring to?" Though she'd guessed, she wanted Richards to be clear on what this mysterious request was all about.

"Vanessa Ainsworth, of course."

"Okay, what about her?"

"It just so happens that Ainsworth is an Indian."

Oh, that again. "So what does that have to do with me?"

Sergeant Guthrie interjected, "Don't drag this out, Detective, just tell her what you want her to do."

Richards didn't look happy about the sergeant's direction, but then he never looked happy about anything. "We've tried to notify her next of kin. The only one we could locate was her ex-husband, Acton Ainsworth. Turns out he's the owner of the Ainsworth Furniture Store chain."

Tempe had heard that Vanessa was well-off because of the divorce settlement she'd received from her ex, but that was all. Tempe still couldn't figure out what this had to do with her. Neither Richards nor Morrison had ever been big on sharing information with her.

"And?" Tempe prompted.

Sergeant Guthrie cupped his square jaw in his meaty hand and rolled his eyes. "Yes, get on with it, please."

Morrison leaned around Richard. "We want you to go to Crescent City."

"What?" Where the heck was Crescent City? She'd heard of it, but had only the foggiest notion of where it was. Somewhere up north, along the coast, she thought.

"The victim's ex seems to think that we need to get in touch with her cousin. He says the cousin is the only one who might have an idea who did this to her. We could get some law-enforcement people up there to question her, but..." Morrison paused.

Richards jumped in. "You've got a way of finding stuff out from Indians."

Tempe shook her head and laughed. "I don't even know what tribe you're talking about. What makes you think I'll have any better luck learning anything than anyone else?"

"Wait a minute here." Sergeant Guthrie leaned forward, his arms on the stack of file folders on his desk. "As I remember, Crabtree, a while back you didn't know a heck of a lot about your own people. That didn't stop you from gaining their confidence and finding out things none of the rest of us could. They accepted you because you were one of them."

"Let's be practical about this. I'm a Yanduchi which is part of the Yokuts. Those are the Indians who live around here. I've known some of them nearly all my life. It won't be the same with people from another tribe," Tempe said.

Richards attempted a pleading expression. With his perpetual squint, he merely succeeded in making himself look comical. "Crabtree, you're our only chance here. Otherwise the investigation is at a standstill. The ex has a solid alibi."

"Have you questioned her former boyfriend, Eric Figueroa? You did know she had a restraining order against him, right?"

Morrison waved a meaty hand. "Yeah, we're looking at him."

Though she didn't think Eric had anything to do with Vanessa's death, he ought to be near the top of the list of suspects. The problem seemed to be the detectives didn't have any suspects.

"Will you do this for us?" Richards asked.

"I still don't understand what it is you want me to do."

"I thought we made it pretty clear. We want you to go to Crescent City and spend some time with the Ainsworth woman's cousin." He pulled a notebook out of the pocket of his T-shirt. After he flipped a few pages, he added, "Her name is Abigail Jacoby." He ripped the page out and handed it to Tempe. "Here's her address and phone number."

Tempe rolled her eyes and sighed. "I can't believe you guys. I can't just up and leave without discussing this with my husband."

"You won't be gone long," Richards said. "We've got an airline ticket for you. You'll fly out of Fresno tomorrow morning. You'll go to San Francisco and from there you'll transfer to a smaller plane to Crescent City. Your return trip will depend on how long it takes you to find out what we need to know." He pulled open his jacket, reached into an inside packet and pulled out a long envelope. "Everything you need is right here. Airline tickets, car rental, cash for meals and a motel. Take civilian clothes. You'll be able to relate better if you're not in uniform. We've already made the proper notification to the airlines and taken care of the necessary red tape so you can carry concealed on board. We've already contacted the sheriff's department up there and they've promised to assist you if you have any problems."

Dumbfounded, Tempe turned to Sergeant Guthrie.

He raised his eyebrows. "Hey, it's a good opportunity for you, Crabtree. It'll look good in your record."

"It may not look so good to my husband." In reality she wondered if he'd notice she was gone. He had his hands full with the evacuees. Even after the fire was out, those who had damaged homes might ask for Hutch's help. Maybe a short separation was exactly what their marriage needed. "Okay, okay. Since it sounds like I really don't have a choice, I'll go."

# CHAPTER FIVE

Before going home, Tempe drove through Bear Creek, past The Café, The Saloon, the Bear Creek Grocery, the Inn, and the fire station. At one time, the businesses may have had more original names but if so, they were long forgotten. When she reached the church, she could see the parking lot was still full of trucks, trailers and campers. A few horses were corralled inside the cemetery fence.

As soon as she climbed out of the Blazer, the evacuees crowded around her, tossing questions.

"What's the latest news about the fire?" an elderly man asked.

Followed by a young woman's question, "Has the road block been lifted?"

"When can we go back home?" was the common theme.

She held up her hands as she hurried through the group toward the open door of the church. "I probably don't know as much as the rest of you. I've been in Dennison this morning on other business. I just stopped by to see my husband. Anyone know where I can find him?"

Mr. Bender, still wearing the same khaki shorts and striped knit shirt from the day before, pointed toward the church. "Pastor Hutch just went inside with more supplies."

Cartons of water bottles, packs of toilet tissue and paper towels were stacked beside the door. Tempe entered and called out, "Hutch, it's me. Where are you?"

Hutch, auburn hair more unruly than usual, poked his

head out the door of the small kitchen near the front of the church. "Hi, honey. You can't believe how busy we've been. The ladies of the church just finished serving lunch for everyone. If you're hungry, I might be able to find a stray tuna sandwich for you." He grinned.

For a moment, all she could think of was how much she loved him. "No, thanks. I haven't the time. I do need to talk to you about something though."

"Of course." Wrinkles furrowed his lightly freckled brow. "What's wrong?"

"It's about Vanessa Ainsworth's murder."

He looked puzzled.

"I told you about it last night."

"Yes, of course. What does it have to do with you? You aren't going to investigate this on your own, are you?"

Tempe nodded. "I'm afraid I am. This time it's the detectives' idea."

He straightened his shoulders and widened his eyes. "That's a switch."

"Yes, I'm surprised too. But, listen, sweetheart, it means I have to go out of town for a few days."

"Out of town? Where?"

"The department is sending me to Crescent City to interview a close relative of Vanessa's."

"Isn't that unusual? Why did they decide you should do it?"

"Because it turns out Vanessa was part Native American, and the detectives think I'll relate better to her cousin than they would."

Hutch ran his fingers through his hair, mussing it even more. "Couldn't you turn them down? Don't they realize you're needed here with the fire and all?"

"Sweetheart, they didn't give me a choice. They're sending a car for me early tomorrow morning. My flight leaves at eight from Fresno."

A plump-faced woman appeared in the doorway. "Pastor Hutch, we need to know what you want us to fix for dinner."

"I'm sorry, honey, I've got to go. Give me a kiss. I'm going to miss you."

Tempe stepped into his embrace. His arms tightened around her and he tipped her face toward his. The kiss he gave her was too brief.

When he released her, he said, "Call me when you arrive. Let me know where I can reach you."

"I wish we had more time to talk."

"Me too. When all this mess is over, we'll make time. Be careful." He caressed her cheek before striding back into the kitchen.

❧❧

At the wheel of her Blazer, Tempe turned on the ignition. Even though she'd just seen Hutch, she missed him terribly. Before all their disagreements about the casino on the reservation, he'd been a wonderful sounding board. He often made her think about things in a new way that surprised her. Lately, he'd buried himself in church activities, ministering to the needy and he hardly had any time for her. Their intimacy had suffered too. Now their lovemaking had become a scheduled event. The spontaneity that had made it so special had disappeared.

She drove away from the church and thought about what she had to do to prepare for her trip. First she'd get on the computer at home, do a search, and see what she could find out about Crescent City. No doubt it was much cooler there than the hundred plus temperatures here that made it so hard on the firefighters.

Driving through town, she spotted Nick Two John's truck in the parking lot of the Inn. On impulse, she turned in and parked next to it. The lot was nearly empty. Claudia Donato's sports car was gone. Claudia owned the Inn and she and Two John were lovers.

The only other two rather dilapidated vehicles belonged to employees. Obviously the fire had discouraged any tourists from an overnight stay.

The Inn was open only for brunch on Sundays, and dinner from Wednesday through Sunday. Hopefully that meant Two John wasn't too busy to talk to her. Tempe began to feel better. Nick Two John, a Yanduchi like Tempe, had amazing and often puzzling insight.

She found Nick in the kitchen overseeing a crew assembling sandwiches and a huge vat of potato salad. Though Nick's expression remained unchanged, he greeted her like he was happy to see her. As usual, he wore his long black hair in two braids that nearly reached his waist. With his bronze complexion and chiseled features, Nick looked as though he'd stepped out of the past. He explained they were making a delivery to the staging area to help feed the firefighters. "We've been helping with meals since the beginning of the fire."

Oh dear, Nick probably wouldn't have time for her either. "Hutch is doing the same for the refugees from the fire. Some of them are camped out in the church parking lot."

"I've heard. Your husband is a good man, Tempe." Nick's dark eyes always seemed to penetrate into Tempe's soul. "You're anxious. How can I help?"

She wasn't about to mention her troubled relationship with Hutch. She'd already spent too many hours talking about the pros and cons of the casino with Nick. His views were a mix of Tempe's and Hutch's. Nick feared the evils of gambling too, but he worried more about a criminal element trying to wiggle its way into the management of the Indian's new venture. So far the Yanduchi in charge had managed to retain control of what was a profitable venture for the Indians.

"Do you have time to talk to me? I can see you're busy, but I've been given an assignment that I'd like to discuss with you."

"Everyone knows what to do." He tossed his truck keys to a young man packing sandwiches in a large cooler. "Soon as you're done, Jake, deliver the food to the staging area. The rest of you, clean up and finish the prep for the dinner menu. Don't bother with much, I doubt we'll have many customers."

He led the way into the cavernous dining room. The Inn

had originally been a stage stop before being enlarged and redesigned with the addition of the modern kitchen and sleeping rooms. The original stone fireplace dominated one wall. Light poured in the lightly curtained windows on the wall nearest the street. Pulling out two chairs from the nearest table, he said, "Tell me about this assignment."

Tempe filled him in on Vanessa Ainsworth's murder.

A cloud passed briefly over Nick's eyes. "Yes, I heard."

"Because she was an Indian, the detectives are sending me to Crescent City to interview her cousin. They seem to think she'll be more open with me because of our shared heritage."

Nick's expression didn't change. "What do you know about the Indians in that part of California?"

"Absolutely nothing. Do you?"

"There are things we have in common with all native people."

"Like what?"

"The government sent us to live in remote places where we were far from needed resources and ways to make a living. You know what it was like before the casino was built. Our people had to drive all the way to Dennison to find jobs, and there weren't many employers willing to hire us."

"Do you know the tribal names of the people where I'm going?" she asked.

"The Yuroks and the Tolowa are native to northwestern California and southern Oregon. In my conversations with Vanessa, I learned she was a Tolowa."

That was a new piece of information. "You talked to Vanessa?"

"Why do you find that surprising?"

"I had no idea she was an Indian until today when the detectives told me."

"You're always too busy to listen."

It was true she was busy, but Tempe always considered herself a good listener. Even exhausted, or bored by a long-winded person, she always forced herself to look interested and paid attention so she'd know how to react, or not to, about what was being reported. Arguing with Nick Two John was a futile exercise. "So how did she happen to tell you about her background?"

"She came to me with a request. A request I turned down."

It was so darn hard to get what you wanted to know out of Nick. "What did she want?"

"To paint my portrait. She said I reminded her of her people, the Tolowa."

This wasn't going to be easy. "What did she have to say about the Tolowa?"

"First, they were nearly wiped out by the white men's diseases. Then the settlers massacred them by the hundreds, the ones who escaped hid in caves in the forest. Today they aren't recognized as an Indian tribe."

"I'm wondering if Vanessa's cousin will even talk to me," Tempe said.

"When you meet her, she'll see that you are one of the native people. She will speak freely to you."

Nodding, Tempe rolled her eyes. "That's what the detectives are counting on."

"It would be easier for you if you were more steeped in your heritage." Nick Two John had always berated her for her lack of knowledge of native ways and beliefs. Anything she had learned or experienced caused hard feelings between her and Hutch. In most cases, he didn't believe Indian spiritualism and Christianity made a good mix, though he'd come to be surprisingly tolerant of Nick. In fact, despite Hutch's stand against the casino, he and Nick's friendship hadn't suffered. Certainly not like Tempe's and Hutch's own relationship.

"I'm the best the department has, or at least the one the detectives are willing to part with for a few days," Tempe said, noting a slight edge to her voice. "That's why I'm here, Nick. If there's anything you can tell me that will help me learn whatever I can from Vanessa's cousin, or anyone else up there in Crescent City, please do. I'm not sure she'll even know anything that will help us to find out who killed Vanessa, but if she does, I sure want to hear it."

"It will be necessary to win her confidence first." Nick's gaze never faltered. He seldom blinked, an unnerving habit Tempe could never get used to.

"What's the best way for me to do that?" She had never had any problem gaining witnesses' confidence on the Bear Creek Reservation. The fact that she was Yanduchi, and looked Indian, had always opened doors for her. But would that make a difference to this Tolowa woman?

"Try to remember what it is like to be a Native American in a hostile environment."

Tempe felt her face flush. The worst times for Tempe as an Indian had been her days in high school when she'd been called "half breed," "red skin" and "squaw." Often she was shunned by the other kids. Even the other Indian teens from the reservation didn't accept her because she'd been raised off the rez by her father who was half Yanduchi and her mother who was an Anglo like the majority of Bear Creek's residents. Her Indian grandmother lived with the family until her death when Tempe was twelve. Nana had told many stories about her life on the reservation. Most of them Tempe had forgotten. Being part Indian hadn't been something Tempe was proud of during her growing-up years. When she married her first husband, Milt Kincaid, they moved to San Diego and she never thought about her Indian roots. When her son Blair was born she was happy he resembled his light-haired father. When Milt died in the line of duty on the job as a highway patrolman, Blair was only two.

She moved back to Bear Creek, living for a time with her parents who cared for Blair while she went to college. Later, she attended the police academy, graduated top of her class and was hired as a deputy. She worked in various jurisdictions around the county. When she was assigned to Bear Creek as resident deputy, so many people called her by her maiden name, it was easier just to use it. Her mother died in an auto accident and her father moved to a retirement community in Arizona. An aunt passed away and left Tempe the small cottage she and Hutch lived in today.

"I'll do my best," Tempe snapped, but was immediately sorry. If it hadn't been for Nick, she wouldn't know as much about her people as she did. "I didn't mean to be cranky. I guess I'm just nervous. I'm going to a place I know nothing about and have to find out what I can about a person I didn't know very well from a perfect stranger. The odds aren't too good, are they?"

The briefest of smiles lifted the corners of Nick's mouth. "The reference to gambling is not appropriate for this situation."

"No, it's not. I suppose I better get home and start packing. I've kept you long enough." Tempe started to rise, but when Nick spoke, she sat again.

"Wisdom only comes when you stop looking for it. Live your life the way the Creator intended. Be concerned for others, not yourself, and you'll find what you're looking for."

Typical Two John advice.

She stood. "Thank you, Nick, I'll do my best."

"Of course you will."

She left Nick standing in the empty dining room. Turning back once to wave, she thought again how much he looked like a Yanduchi from the past, his face shadowed, his long braids hanging down over his shirt.

≈≈

At home, she went into her bedroom, pulled a chair up to the computer on her desk and did a search for Crescent City. She wanted to know what kind of weather to expect and a little about the area.

As she'd guessed, Crescent City was located on the ocean and bordered Oregon. Though the Yuroks and Tolowa tribes were mentioned on the website, there was nothing about the massacres Nick had mentioned. Instead, it said that both tribes had adapted to the community and pursued their livings in the fishing and lumber industries.

The website told of shipwrecks from 1850 to an oil tanker fired upon by a Japanese submarine in 1941. Interesting fact.

After learning a bit more about Crescent City, Tempe resisted the urge to look up anything more about the Tolowa people. It would be best to find out about them from Vanessa's cousin, Abigail Jacoby. At least it would give Tempe something to ask the woman about.

⁓≈

The trip to San Francisco was uneventful, though it was a bit disconcerting when the airplane descended through the clouds and made its low approach over the water. Tempe couldn't hold back a sigh of relief when the aircraft actually neared a landing strip. Once inside the huge airport, she learned she had to hurry almost to the opposite end of the sprawling complex to catch the plane to Crescent City. There was little time to do it.

When she arrived at the proper gate, the last of the passengers disappeared inside the door. She presented her boarding pass to the attendant, stepped inside, and was surprised to see a staircase. Lifting her carry-on bag, she hurried down after the man in front of her. Once outside, she tagged along behind the others on a marked lane on the tarmac to a waiting plane. This one was much smaller than the one she'd been on previously. In fact, it was the smallest plane she'd ever flown in.

Oh well, a new adventure for a small town deputy. Tempe found her seat easily and was glad no one sat next to her. Once everyone was seat-belted, the plane taxied toward the runway. No others seemed the least dismayed about the size of the plane as evidenced by the happy sounding chatter of strangers getting acquainted with their seatmates, so Tempe tried to relax. It seemed that no sooner did the aircraft start down the runway than it was airborne.

Tempe had hoped to see the changing coastline from the window, but soon clouds obscured her view. Instead, she passed the time thinking about the task that lay ahead. She wondered how she would be received by Abigail Jacoby. Would the woman even know anything helpful about Vanessa that could lead to her killer? Tempe knew very little about Vanessa, and they'd lived in the same area for at least three years. How would the Del Norte County Sheriff's Department in Crescent City view her visit to their territory? Would they think of her as some sort of oddity? Or perhaps something worse?

An even more disturbing thought crossed Tempe's mind. Did Abigail Jacoby know she was coming? Had anyone broken the news to this woman about the death of her cousin?

# CHAPTER 6

McNamara Field in Crescent City was so small it hardly looked like an airport. Landing there was a bit scary as the plane descended into patchy fog. Obviously the rest of the passengers had made this trip before. As they gathered their possessions and exited the aircraft, they all seemed to know where to go. Tempe followed along behind. She peered around while waiting for her other suitcase to be retrieved from the plane, trying to locate the rental car desk.

Finally she asked someone who she thought might know. He grinned and pointed outside.

She wasn't exactly sure what that meant. But once she had her luggage, she stepped through the main entrance and discovered the rental car company in a small building across the parking lot. Surprisingly, the attendant pointed out the car that was waiting for her, a light blue, midsize Ford sedan.

Once she'd signed all the papers, she asked for directions to the sheriff's department.

The clerk, a young woman with a blond pony tail, obligingly unfolded a map of the local area. She pointed out the airport and ran her finger down what looked like one of the main streets. "You really can't miss it. When you reach the road, turn left. Go straight ahead and it's on the left hand side." She described some landmarks to watch for.

After stowing her belongings in the back seat of the sedan, Tempe followed the directions given to her. First she passed rather large, expensive homes, but the neighborhood quickly changed to smaller houses, some neglected, others carefully kept.

She spotted the small skate park the clerk had told her about. Next to it was a fenced lot with patrol cars and boats on trailers parked inside. The building that housed the department was gray with blue trim and a flag pole stood in front. The place had a much friendlier aura than the building that housed her sub-station.

Inside, she was greeted by a plump, female dispatcher. "May I help you?"

Tempe pulled out her wallet and displayed her identification. "I'm Deputy Tempe Crabtree from Bear Creek."

The woman grinned broadly, exposing slightly bucked teeth. "Yes, Deputy, you're expected." She opened an inside door, and ushered Tempe through. "Sergeant Glade's office is at the end of the corridor."

Once the dispatcher returned to her post, she must have alerted the Sergeant. Before Tempe reached her destination, a tall, slim man with a shaved head stepped out through the last doorway.

"Deputy Crabtree, welcome to Crescent City. I'm Jeff Glade. Come in and take a seat."

Glade's office was larger and neater than Sergeant Guthrie's. He had interesting framed photographs of himself hanging on what seemed to be freshly painted walls. In one he was holding a gigantic fish. Another showed him, rifle in hand, beside a large buck lying on the ground. Before she could study any others, the Sergeant asked, "How best can we facilitate your visit here?"

"Since I'm here to interview Ms. Abigail Jacoby, directions to her house would be helpful."

It was difficult for Tempe to guess Sergeant Glade's age. He was deeply tanned, and obviously spent a good deal of time outdoors. Except for a few lines around his eyes, his facial skin was smooth and he had no age spots on his hands folded on the top of his clean desk.

"We haven't alerted Ms. Jacoby about your visit."

"Does that mean that no one has told her about the death of her cousin?"

"We haven't. I don't know about your office."

Terrific. She was the one who was going to break the news. It wouldn't help her situation here to complain. Instead, she asked, "If there's anything you can tell me about Ms. Jacoby, I'd certainly appreciate it."

Sergeant Glade scrutinized Tempe for a moment. "I suspect you two will hit it off. She's an Indian too."

Not that again. Tempe wished she'd ignored the detectives' advice not to wear her uniform. She suddenly felt uncomfortable with her black braid hanging down the back of her teal suede jacket that she wore over a simple black T-shirt and black jeans. "I hope so. However, I know very little about the Tolowa people."

The Sergeant's expression changed slightly. Tempe wasn't sure what that meant.

"I can assure you that Abigail will certainly increase your knowledge about the Tolowa and all their troubles." The Sergeant opened his desk drawer and pulled out a newspaper. "Thought you ought to take a look at this. Might give you some insight into the type of woman you'll be dealing with." He slid the newspaper across the desk.

The paper was dated several months earlier. On the front page was a photograph of a formidable woman with a leather head band securing long, light hair, dressed in a simple native outfit. The headline read, "Tolowa Woman Taking on the Government." The story went on to relate that Native American, Abigail Jacoby, had launched a campaign to gain more rights for the Tolowa people. The article urged fellow Tolowa to join her fight.

Before Tempe could read to the end, Sergeant Glade snatched it back, dropped the paper into the drawer and slammed it shut.

"I suppose you could call Ms. Jacoby a political activist. She's a pain in the butt to me because she's always riling up the local Indians about one thing or another. You'd think with all the Indian casinos around here, she'd realize the Indians are getting back what we took from them a nickel at a time."

"It sounds like her issue is totally different," Tempe said quietly.

The look the Sergeant gave her this time was easy to read—he thought she was going to be trouble too. "Your Ms. Jacoby and her friends have so many issues I can't even remember them all, much less tell you about them." He shoved his chair back and stood. "Go back out to Becky and she'll let you know how to find Ms. Jacoby's house. She'll also give you her phone number. You do have a cell phone, don't you?"

"Actually I don't. Where I live and work in the mountains, the signals are blocked. Cell phones don't work there. Couldn't see any point of buying one."

"Just ask Becky. She'll get you an outside line. If you need any help, just give me a call." He shoved a card at her that Tempe pocketed. The Sergeant was already sitting down and reaching for his phone. She'd been dismissed.

❧❧

The dispatcher, Becky, had a marked map ready for Tempe. She kindly offered the phone and Ms. Jacoby's phone number. After all this, it would be just Tempe's luck that the woman would be away from home.

Fortunately, the phone was answered after three rings by an authoritative female voice. "Abigail Jacoby here, how may I help you?"

"Ms. Jacoby, this is Deputy Tempe Crabtree from Bear Creek. I was a friend of your cousin, Vanessa Ainsworth."

There was a long silence. "You said 'was'. Does that mean you have something bad to tell me about Vanessa?"

"Yes, ma'am, I do. I'm here in Crescent City. Could I come to see you? There's quite a bit I need to talk to you about."

"Come ahead. I'll be waiting." She hung up.

❧❧

According to the map, the directions to Ms. Abigail

Jacoby's home led away from Crescent City. As the road wound around, Tempe was surprised to see huge coastal redwoods. No doubt when the Tolowa first lived in this area, the forest went all the way to the ocean. Though the magnificent trees still marched elegantly up the hillsides, it was only too obvious that many had been cleared to build homes.

She rounded a corner and was surprised to see a brightly painted casino. Unlike the Bear Mountain Casino, which was tucked into a hidden valley on reservation grounds, this casino had access right off the highway. Its parking lot was nearly filled with cars, trucks, a few motor homes, travel trailers, fifth-wheelers and several tourist buses.

Still following the directions, Tempe turned the car off the main thoroughfare onto a narrow paved street heading toward the tree-covered mountains. She had to glance at her map several times, as the yellow marker guided her to turn off one road and onto another and she guided her car through the maze.

*It'll be a wonder if I find my way out of here.*

Most of the houses were small, tucked away among the natural foliage of the area. Rhododendron grew wild among the redwoods that surrounded the homes. What a gorgeous place to live.

She found the number she was looking for on the mailbox. The house itself was nearly hidden by the natural growth around it, including purple and lavender wildflowers Tempe had never seen before. She drove up the dirt lane and saw that the house was constructed of redwood planks and resembled a cabin. A carport, attached to the left side of the home, sheltered an old gray Nissan sedan.

Before she could climb out of the rental car, the yellow front door opened wide. A heavy-set, middle-aged woman stepped out on a broad porch to greet Tempe. Her long hair, that was dark at the bottom but gray then silvered at the roots, was combed back from the broad, bronze face and held with large barrettes decorated with turquoise and coral stones. She wore a simple lavender tunic, and a long multi-colored broomstick skirt. In comfortable-looking moccasins, she moved toward Tempe. The woman's eyes narrowed and scrutinized Tempe.

Holding out her hand, Tempe said, "I'm Deputy Tempe Crabtree."

The woman's grasp was warm and strong. "I didn't expect you to be Indian. Which tribe to you belong to?"

"My people are Yanduchi, part of the Yokuts," Tempe said.

"Do you live on the reservation?"

"No, ma'am. I'm the resident deputy for the town of Bear Creek and the outlying areas. However, I do know many of the people from the rez."

"Come in, and please, don't call me ma'am any more. Abby is what most people call me."

"And I'm Tempe."

Abby held the door open and Tempe stepped inside the living room. Though small, it was warm and inviting. Sunshine filtered through the heavy growth and into the window on the side of the house opposite the carport. The thick trunk of a redwood was visible in the background.

"What a lovely place," Tempe said.

"I don't think you came here to judge my home." A bit of hostility had crept into Abby's voice. She folded her arms across her ample bosom. "Why don't you take a seat and tell me the purpose of your visit?" She settled herself in a hand-carved redwood chair with brightly colored cushions.

Tempe perched on the edge of a worn but comfortable couch. A fleece throw with a wolf design on it was tossed across the back and wooden arm.

"It's about your cousin, Vanessa Ainsworth."

"Something's happened to her, hasn't it?"

"Yes, ma'am…Abigail…Abby. There was a forest fire in Bear Creek. In fact, it was still burning when I left. Your cousin's body was found in the remains of her burned studio."

Horror distorted Abby's face. "She burned to death?"

"No, someone shot her. We think it happened sometime before the fire."

Abby shook her head. "My Lord. I knew it had to be something bad for you to come all the way up here to tell me about her." Tears streamed down her cheeks. "I expected something like this. I thought I'd prepared myself. Guess I was wrong."

Tempe reached over and patted Abigail's hand. "The news is shocking, I know. It's always hard to lose someone."

Pulling a tissue from a pocket in her tunic, Abby wiped her eyes and nose. "Vanessa and I grew up together. Her mother died when she was young and her father had a drinking problem. Our mothers were sisters. My parents brought her home right after my aunt's funeral. I was a change-of-life baby and my older brothers and sisters were all grown and out on their own. Vanessa and I shared parents, a room, friends, ambitions and secrets. She was much closer to me than any of my real siblings."

Tempe nodded. She was glad to hear this about the two women's relationship. It was possible that Abby might have some knowledge that would lead to the identity of Vanessa's murderer.

"Do you know who shot her?" Abby asked.

"No, I'm afraid we don't."

"And that's why you're here. You're hoping I'll know who did it."

"That's why I was sent here," Tempe admitted.

"I'm sorry to disappoint you, but I don't see how I can help."

# CHAPTER SEVEN

Tempe's heart sank. She should have known it wouldn't be easy. Her hope, though not realistic, had been that once Abby heard about Vanessa that she'd immediately give her the name of the murderer along with the motive.

"How long will you be around?" Abby asked.

"I don't know. Besides delivering the sad news about your cousin's death, my assignment is to find out whatever I can about Vanessa."

"Where are you staying?" Abby asked.

"I don't know that either. I suppose I'll find a motel some-where in town."

Abby stood. "Goodness no, you'll stay here with me."

"You don't even know me. I don't want to impose on you."

"I know that you're taking the time to learn what you can about Vanessa to bring her murderer to justice. That's enough for me. Truly, I don't know if anything I can tell you will help, but talking about Vanessa will certainly help me with my grief."

It would be much easier to be with Abby as she thought about her cousin and their life together growing up and any-thing else she cared to share about Vanessa. "Okay, if you're sure you want to do this."

"Of course I do. I have a few obligations. If you don't mind, you can come along with me. I'll also have to pass the news about Vanessa along to some of her friends. I'm glad my parents are no longer with us. Bring your luggage in."

᠕᠊᠊ᠷᡅᠬᡄᠨᠷ

Before Tempe had a chance to take in the details of the tiny but comfortable looking guestroom, Abby said, "If you'd like to come with me, I'm going to visit a friend, Vanessa's and mine, at the Gushu Teahouse and Galleria."

Tempe's offer to take the rental car was accepted. Expecting their destination to be in a shopping mall of some sort, she was startled when she was directed to drive into another small community that Abby identified as Smith River and turned up a sparsely settled side street.

She pointed out a small redwood structure resembling a church. "Park in front."

There wasn't a parking lot, just a grassy lawn that ran into the asphalt of the road. Tempe laughed, "This isn't anything like I expected."

"You'll be even more amazed when you meet our hostess, Justine Mahoney."

Tempe didn't have to wait long. Before they were even out of the car, a tall, stately woman with a broad smiling face, wisps of salt and pepper hair falling across her smooth forehead, stepped onto the porch and leaned on the railing.

"Abby, I've been waiting for you. And who is this you've brought with you?"

As Tempe neared the porch she noticed the woman had three vertical tattooed lines below her mouth to the bottom of her chin. *Wonder what that's all about?*

Abby hurried ahead and gave Ms. Mahoney a big hug that was reciprocated. When they'd finished their exuberant greeting, Abby said, "I have sad news about Vanessa. I'll let my new friend, Tempe Crabtree, tell you about what happened."

"Hi." Tempe smiled at Ms. Mahoney.

When Tempe reached the woman, she wrapped Tempe in a big bear hug too. Upon releasing her, she pushed the door of the teahouse open wide. "I'm Justine. Come on inside. Have some of my killer coffee and a cookie. Or you can have tea. I have all kinds, including native teas."

The interior of the building looked even more like a

church but on a diminutive scale. On the left was a glassed-in counter filled with what looked like hand-crafted gift items. Displayed on the wall were hand crocheted hats of many colors. The kitchen was straight ahead, but the main part of the room had simple redwood benches lining the wall and a small stage at one end with a doorway on either side. Several mismatched tables and chairs were scattered around. Framed paintings hung on the wall.

Tempe noticed a brightly colored abstract painting of a Pow Wow. Something about it looked familiar. She stepped closer to read the signature at the bottom. Vanessa Ainsworth. "Oh, this is one of Vanessa's paintings."

"Yes. It's one of the few she did that has a tie to her heritage," Justine Mahoney said as she carried a tray to a table spread with a red-checked table cloth. On the tray were three steaming mugs of different colors and shapes, paper napkins, spoons, and honey. "I made this coffee myself. You'll like it. Now tell me about Vanessa."

Tempe joined the other women at the table. "I'm a deputy from Bear Creek."

Justine's dark eyes opened wide, glistening with tears.

"It's hard to be the one to bring bad news, but the best way to do this is just come out with it. Vanessa Ainsworth was murdered."

Sniffing, Justine said, "I wish I could have seen her one last time. It's been so long since she visited. I can't believe she's gone." She scowled. "Who did it? That scummy ex-husband of hers?"

"We don't know who did it and her former husband has an alibi. That's the reason I was sent up here, to see if I could learn anything that would help the detectives on the case find out who the killer is." Tempe absently picked up her cup and blew on the hot liquid. A rich scent wafted from it. "I think the detectives are hoping that something from her past might be linked to her murder."

"I can't think of anything," Abby said. "Can you?"

Justine shook her head.

"Perhaps if you two would just tell me about Vanessa. What was she like when she lived here?"

"We all grew up together in Lake Earl. We attended school together. We're the first generation of Tolowa that wasn't hauled off to boarding school," Justine said.

Abby said, "That was the white's way of trying to sanitize the native children. They cut off their hair and made sure they spoke only English. No wonder most of our people can't speak their native language."

This was something else Tempe had never heard about.

"Can you speak the language of your people?" Justine asked.

Tempe shook her head. "I know that there are a few women on the rez who are teaching the children the old ways and the language."

"Do you live on the reservation?" Justine pulled her red sweater tighter around her slim torso.

"No, I never have. Unfortunately, I never really learned much about my heritage until the last few years."

"Humph. Don't tell me you were like Vanessa, ashamed of your Indian blood," Justine said.

Tempe lowered her head and sipped the coffee. "When I was growing up I was made fun of for being an Indian. The kids called me names. I hated being an Indian. It made me feel bad though, because my grandmother was an Indian. She lived with us and I loved her dearly."

"Vanessa had the reverse problem. Most of the kids at school were Tolowa or Yurok. She got teased because she didn't look like an Indian. Her father was a white man with blonde hair. She took after him. She could hardly wait to get away from here," Abigail said.

Justine laughed. "And I was the opposite, I couldn't stay away. I went to school at Chico State and earned my bachelor's degree in art. Did a few years of graduate studies too. But I had to come back home."

Tempe glanced around the room at the other paintings. "Are some of these yours?"

"Oh yes, quite a few. Mine are the ones that are matted but not framed."

"Justine's political views as they apply to Indian affairs are apparent in many of her paintings. She's passionate about them, and vocal, just as I am." Abby fixed her gaze on Justine.

"That's a good description of both of us," Justine said. "What do you know about the Tolowa?"

"Very little."

Justine's eyes darkened until her pupils weren't distinguishable from the iris. "I've been outspoken because for many years we weren't even recognized by the government as a tribe. Though that was finally changed, it's far too little. It certainly doesn't make up for the fact that the white people tried to kill us all. If some hadn't hidden in the forest, there'd be none of us left today." She pointed to the marks on her chin. "This is the tribal marking 111 which honors my connection to the people we come from. Let me tell you about the history of my people."

Abby glanced at her watch, but Justine ignored her gesture.

Though she doubted what she was about to hear would help her to learn anything that would help find Vanessa's killer, Tempe could tell that Justine was indeed zealous about the subject and nothing could stop her now.

# CHAPTER EIGHT

Justine began her story with, "Just imagine what life might have been like when the Tolowa lived in permanent, year-round villages, when the big trees went all the way to the ocean. They built their houses and canoes out of redwood. Fishing was great. Plenty of salmon and sturgeon and all the good things from the ocean, plus an abundance of deer and elk."

"What does Tolowa mean?" Tempe asked.

Justine laughed. "When the Yurok were asked who we were, they said *tolowa* which means the people from over there, and the name stuck."

"Sounds like it was a good time for the Indians back then," Tempe said.

"It was until the white man came." Justine crossed her arms and above the tattoo, her lips became a straight line.

"Really, it's a wonder there are any of us left with all the massacres that went on," Abby said. "But Tempe didn't come here to learn about our people. She wants to find out about Vanessa."

"Really, it's okay," Tempe said. "I'll listen to whatever you have to say."

Glaring at Abby, Justine said. "I know why she's here. But don't you think she at least ought to have a clue about the battles that we've been fighting these days?"

Abby shrugged.

Frowning, Tempe asked, "I don't understand what you mean."

Sitting straighter in her chair, Justine continued. "We've been to court to try and get our Indian cemeteries and village sites recognized and preserved but to no avail. If it's not one thing it's another. The last time the court lost our brief. The judge sided with the environmentalists and the Fish and Game people."

With her tattoo and assertive personality, Justine would be a formidable opponent. Tempe wouldn't want to come up against her no matter the cause. "You'd think that the environmentalists would be on the side of the Indians."

"That's a laugh. A lot of what's happening to our people isn't right." After a huge sigh, Justine picked up her mug and sipped her coffee. "Darn, it's nearly cold. I'll get more." She pushed back her chair and went to the kitchen.

"Have patience," Abby said, "She'll eventually get around to Vanessa."

"I don't mind."

Tempe smiled at Justine when she brought in the pot and topped off everyone's coffee. A rich aroma rose from the cups. "You're right, the coffee is delicious."

"I know you didn't come all the way up here to learn about the Tolowa, but I want everyone to know what happened to my people." Justine sat down and picked up her cup and held it thoughtfully.

"What else do you think I should know about the Tolowa?" Tempe suspected that the more interest she showed in what Justine wanted to tell her, the more willing she'd be to talk about Vanessa.

Abby rolled her eyes.

Justine scowled at her old friend before turning her attention to Tempe and continuing, "Not only were they murdered in great numbers, the few who were left were shuffled around to one reservation after another. And the worst came when the Feds banned all the Indian religions."

That was something else Tempe had never heard. She glanced around the building. "This place kind of looks like a church. What does Gushu mean? Is it the name of a religion?"

Justine laughed. "Not exactly, but yes, the Tolowa built this for a church in 1928. The word *gushu* means redwood."

"And as you can see redwood was used to build it," Abby added.

Justine broke in with, "We built it, but we still have to pay taxes on it."

"What kind of church was it?" Tempe asked.

"A Shaker church," Abby said.

That was puzzling. "Shaker?" She had heard about them, but thought they were somewhere in the Midwest. "Don't they make furniture too?"

Justine laughed. "Not those Shakers. The Indian Shaker Church took a bit from the Catholics and the Protestants and mixed it up with native spiritualism. People actually shaking when they worship is what gave the religion its name."

"Missionaries and Indian agents tried to abolish the movement, but the Shaker faith became quite popular. It's still active in a few places," Abby answered.

"Now the Gushu Teahouse and Galleria is a community art gallery. We have Friday night jams, monthly receptions, lectures, and story telling events. All family inspired, alcohol, drug and tobacco free events," Justine said, proudly.

"I'm getting hungry. Why don't we head over to the casino and eat?" Abby said.

"Not me." Justine said. "I'm not going there."

"Oops, I forgot. Don't let her get started on how she feels about casinos. Tell you what, Justine. We're going to eat. If you think of anything about Vanessa that might help Tempe, give me a call. We'll get together again. Come over to the house later tonight if you feel like it."

Tempe stood. "Thank you so much, Justine."

"Except for the coffee, I don't think I gave you anything to thank me for."

"Actually, I found what you told me very interesting."

꩜꩜

Like the casino on the Bear Creek reservation, the food at

this one was excellent—and Tempe was hungry. Neither she nor Abby had much to say until their plates were nearly empty. When Abby shoved her plate away, she said, "You have to understand about Justine. As you could probably tell, she's even more passionate than I am about anything that has to do with the Tolowa.

"Standing up for your people is certainly commendable," Tempe said, feeling a tad guilty because she'd never even felt it necessary to stand up for the Yokuts or any other Indians, except as individuals.

Abby shook her head. "You didn't come here to listen to all our political views about the Tolowa. We ought to be talking about what brought you all the way up here to meet me."

"I don't mind listening to what you have to say about making life for the Tolowa better."

"Jitter and I both expend a lot of energy trying to make changes that will help our people."

Tempe grabbed the bill as soon as the waitress put it on the table. "This is on the Tulare County Sheriff's Department."

She felt someone's eyes upon her, and glanced around. Just as she did, she spotted a man ducking behind a wall. Probably just a coincidence. She didn't know anyone in Crescent City or Smith River, or wherever the heck she was.

As she and Abby left the casino, Tempe peered here and there, watching for any furtive movements. It was nearly dark. Despite the bright lights of the casino, plenty of hiding places were in the dark shadows created by the parked vehicles.

"Is something wrong?" Abby asked.

"No. I don't think so." But she couldn't shake the uneasy feeling that someone was watching them.

≈≈

Tempe settled in the corner of Abby's couch while the other woman sat among the pillows on the wooden chair. She turned down the offer of more coffee, still feeling overfull from the generous portions of the meal she'd eaten. Now she had time to enjoy Abby's decorations that added to the ambience.

Woven baskets much like those she'd seen in homes on the Bear Creek Reservation sat in corners and on the small tables scattered around the room. A large painting with the bright colors that Vanessa always used was prominently displayed over the mantel of the small brick fireplace.

Abby followed Tempe's gaze. "Yes, that's one of Vanessa's too." She was silent for a moment. "You must think we aren't affected by her death."

"Not at all. You really haven't had time for the news to sink in."

"Neither Justine nor I have seen Vanessa for several years. The last time she was here was right after she divorced her husband."

"What can you tell me about that?"

"Perhaps I should begin even earlier."

"Tell me about her any way you like."

The two lamps on tables at either end of the couch cast pale illumination on Abby's face, heightening her high cheek-bones and aquiline nose as she began her story.

"Vanessa's artistic talent became evident as soon as she put pencil to paper. It was the same for Justine. That's what drew the two together. They were fast friends in grammar school." She chuckled. "Made me a bit jealous. I couldn't draw anything. They were always being asked to make posters for all kinds of events and they painted murals on the inside walls at school."

She continued to talk about what Vanessa did at school. When the girls went on to high school in Crescent City, Vanessa was accepted by the non-native teens because of her fair skin and light hair. Her artistic abilities helped with her social contacts. She was invited to join some of the clubs on campus where the more popular girls were members. Abby and Justine were left out. Though the girls remained good friends, Vanessa's social life became separate from the other two.

All three girls went to different colleges. Vanessa had a full scholarship in art to the University of California at Santa Barbara. When she came home on holiday, she told Abby proudly, "No one at school even knows I'm an Indian."

She minored in business, and went to work in one of the Ainsworth Furniture stores as a bookkeeper where she eventually met the owner, Acton Ainsworth.

A car in obvious need of a tune-up came to a stop in front of the house, interrupting Vanessa's story. "That's Justine. I knew she wouldn't be able to stay away."

From outside, Justine hollered, "Hey, what're you doing there?"

Tempe jumped up, ran to the door and flung it open. "What's going on?" She was just in time to see a tall figure darting into the redwoods.

Waving her arms, Justine said, "Some creep was peeking in the window."

# CHAPTER NINE

"Come on, let's go after him." Justine was poised to run, with one foot already on the first step of the porch.

"No, I don't have any jurisdiction here," Tempe said. "We could call the local law, I suppose."

"Ha. By the time they send someone, he'll be long gone," Justine said, obviously disappointed.

Tempe squinted into the darkness. She couldn't see anyone but could hear something crashing through the thick underbrush."Come inside and describe who you saw and what he was doing."

"I still think we could catch him if we tried." Justine wore the jeans she'd had on before but had topped them with a long, dark blue sweatshirt. Her hair was tied back with a length of thick blue yarn. Obviously disappointed, she followed Tempe into the house.

Plopping down on the couch, she said, "Hi Abby. What's been going on that's interesting enough for a Peeping Tom?"

"Nothing. I've been telling Tempe about our growing up with Vanessa. I just finished with the story about Vanessa meeting Acton at the furniture store." Abby hesitated, before asking, "Are you sure you really saw someone out there?"

"Of course I did. Just as I drove up, my headlights caught this guy with his nose practically pressed to the window. As soon as he spotted the car, he turned and ran."

Tempe leaned toward her. "Could you see what he looked like?"

"Not really, just that he was big. Hey, maybe it was Bigfoot."

"Bigfoot? You're kidding, right?" Tempe said.

"There really is a Bigfoot—lots of them, actually," Justine said.

"Have you ever seen one?" Tempe asked.

"No, but there have been many sightings around here." Justine crossed her arms again, a gesture Tempe realized meant the Tolowa woman was on the offensive.

Abby smiled. "All of us around here believe in Bigfoot. There've been too many who have seen them. Even folks who aren't Indians. But that's not who was peeking in my window, was it?"

"Probably not. The guy was tall, but not big enough for a Bigfoot. Besides the peeper wore clothes."

Though Tempe wasn't willing to accept the Bigfoot story, it didn't matter, it wasn't relevant to her immediate task. "What else can you tell me about this person?"

"I only saw him for about a minute before he took off. Couldn't tell if he was an Indian or not. I think he did have dark hair though, and he was wearing dark clothing. Looked like a long, black coat."

Smart, if you meant to be snooping around in the dark. "Anything else you remember about him?"

"No, he didn't hang around long enough."

"Abby, is there any reason why someone might be spying on you?"

She shook her head. "Not that I know of."

"While we were in the casino restaurant, I had this feeling that someone was watching us. I thought I saw someone duck behind a wall when I looked around. I had the same feeling when we went into the parking lot."

"Sounds like it's someone who's interested in you and what you're doing," Justine said.

"Sergeant Glade, his dispatcher, and you two are the only ones who know I'm here," Tempe said.

Abby and Justine both bent over with laughter.

"What's so funny?" Tempe asked.

"You're from a small town. You ought to know how fast news travels. No doubt Sergeant Glade told all his deputies about you and everyone told their wives. No telling how many people the dispatcher has passed the word to," Abby said. "And I'm sure no one forgot to mention you're an Indian."

Justine could hardly control her giggles in order to speak. "I've been on the phone ever since you left, telling people about Vanessa."

"Even so, why would someone want to spy on me, if that's what was happening?" Tempe asked.

"Could just be curiosity," Abby said. "Why don't I make us a pot of coffee? Anyone hungry? I made a coffee cake this morning that would taste pretty good about now."

"Make it decaf and I'll take you up on it. I'll even give you a hand." Justine followed Abby into her small kitchen.

Tempe could see and hear them as they bustled about.

"Did you tell Tempe about the two fellows from here who fought over Vanessa all through high school and even after she went to college?" Justine asked as she cut Abby's coffee cake and dished it up onto dessert plates.

"No, didn't think about that. You can tell her."

After the cake and coffee was served, Justine continued Vanessa's story between bites and sips.

"All through school, lots of guys went after Vanessa, Indians and whites. All the popular fellows asked her out and she did go, with several of them. She even went steady with one of the football players for nearly a year. Folks around here expected them to get married one day. His name was Rusty Lamereux. Vanessa broke off with him because she said he was getting too serious and his parents weren't thrilled with the fact that she was Tolowa, whether she looked it or not. He was broken-hearted. Then she took up with Jim Wyrick. He was Yurok. Rusty's friends gave Jim a hard time. Even beat him up more than once. Vanessa ended that. More to protect Rusty than anything else."

Abby nodded. "You're exactly right about that. She felt

sorry for Rusty but knew he would be better off with a broken heart than a broken head."

"Do you think either these Romeos might have anything to do with Vanessa's death?"

Both women frowned and stared at each other quizzically.

"I doubt it. Rusty went away to school too. Not sure where. Heard he married and became a football coach somewhere in the Midwest," Abby said.

"Jim's still around. He's married with a bunch of kids. Had a serious drinking problem. Spent some time in jail, been in rehab a couple of times. Last I heard he was doing fairly well. He's clean and even has a regular job."

While the women talked, Tempe ate the delicious cake and drank her coffee. Nothing they'd mentioned gave her a clue as to what might have happened to Vanessa. They continued with anecdotes about their high school days, some funny, others poignant. At times the women's voices choked with emotion and they wiped away tears. Tempe was learning a lot about Vanessa but nothing that sounded like clues that would lead to her killer.

"Oh, I just thought of something. Remember Lanny Hargrove?" Abby asked.

Justine said, "Sure. That nerdy guy who had such a big crush on Vanessa all through high school."

"Nowadays he'd be called a stalker. He was a real pain to Vanessa. Turned up everywhere she went. He even went to UCSB when she was there. He got more and more assertive as time went on."

"Obnoxious is what he was."

Maybe they were on to something. "Did Vanessa ever think he was a threat to her?"

Justine turned to Abby. "You'll have to tell Tempe about that. After Vanessa went to college I didn't hear from her much, except when she came back for a visit and those were more infrequent as time went on. I was away at college too. I can't remember the last time she was here."

"Let me think. She did say he left her notes and gifts at the apartment she shared with three other students. He called a lot, but she just hung up on him. She said he seemed to know where she was going because he always seemed to be there, whether it was the university's library or when she was out on a date with someone at a nice restaurant. I know he irritated her because she complained about him a lot." Abby pondered for a few more moments.

"Oh, there is one more thing. After she started dating Acton, Lanny continued to make a pest of himself. Acton insisted Vanessa file a complaint against Lanny with the police department."

"Did that help?" Tempe asked.

"Not immediately. I think she called the cops on him a couple of times, and once he got arrested and thrown in jail overnight."

"Knowing Vanessa I'm surprised she didn't bail him out," Justine said, laughing.

Abby shook her head. "No, by this time Lanny had become such a problem I think she was actually afraid of him."

"What happened after that?" Tempe asked.

"I don't know whether or not the jail time discouraged Lanny. It wasn't long after that Vanessa graduated from the university with honors. She and Acton flew to Las Vegas to be married. I was disappointed that none of her old friends were invited, but she said they made their decision to marry on the spur of the moment and didn't really tell anyone ahead of time. They had strangers for witnesses."

"That doesn't sound like Vanessa, and I thought so when I heard about the wedding." Justine glanced at her watch and stood. "It's time for me to get on home. I've got lots to do tomorrow. It's been nice talking to you, Tempe." She hugged Tempe first, then Abby, and left.

Tempe helped Abby gather the dishes and cups and take them to the kitchen.

"I'll finish in here. I imagine you'd like to get some rest now. Fresh towels are in the bathroom. Go ahead and take a shower, if you like. And I'll see you in the morning."

The shower and the bed welcomed Tempe. She thought only briefly about what she'd learned about Vanessa. She wanted to find out more about Lanny Hargrove and Vanessa's marriage to Acton Ainsworth, but her last thoughts before she fell asleep were about the mysterious person who had been spying on them.

# CHAPTER 10

Tempe woke to the smell of freshly perked coffee and bacon frying—and a horrible thought. She hadn't called Hutch to let him know she arrived in Crescent City safely. As soon as she dressed she'd rectify that.

Donning her black jeans, she pulled on a rose colored sweater. After putting on her shoulder holster, she slipped into a loose fitting jacket to cover it and her gun. She washed and brushed her hair, fashioning it into her usual single braid.

In the kitchen, she greeted Abby. "Something smells wonderful in here."

"Thought we'd eat hearty. I'm guessing there are some people you'd like to talk to. I've freed up my schedule so I can show you around."

"Thanks, but first I need to make a couple of long distance phone calls, if I may. I know it sounds odd, but I don't have a cell phone. We can't get a signal where I live and work because of the mountains. I'll charge them to my home."

"Help yourself. You can go in the living room where you'll have more privacy." Abby handed her the portable phone from the charger.

Tempe stepped back into the living room and dialed her home phone number. It rang five times and then the answering machine picked up. She glanced at her watch. It was nearly eight. Hutch must already be at the church. She left a short message, apologizing for not calling the day before and gave him Abby's phone number. Then she called the church. His office phone rang several times before a harried female voice answered, "Bear Creek Community Church. This is Mrs. Johnson."

"Hi, this is Pastor Hutch's wife, Tempe. Is he there?"

"Oh, hi, Deputy. He was here a few minutes ago, but I'm afraid he's gone up the mountain to help some people who had some fire damage to their house and belongings. The evacuees have all gone home now. I'm here with some of the other women cleaning up the church."

"Is the fire out?"

"Mostly. They are just mopping up now and watching for hot spots."

"Glad to hear it. Would you leave a note for Hutch and tell him that I arrived safely in Crescent City and I'm staying with Abigail Jacoby. Tell him he can reach me at this number, though I'll probably be out most of the day." She gave Mrs. Johnson the number on the phone and waited while she repeated it. "Let him know I'll call him at home this evening."

The next call she made was to Sergeant Guthrie in Dennison. He answered on the first ring. After she identified herself, he growled, "It's about time, Crabtree. Are you finding out anything useful?"

"I've learned a lot about the victim and people she's known over the years, but I don't know how useful any of it is. I plan to talk to some more people today. I'm staying with Vanessa's cousin, Ms. Jacoby." She gave him Abby's number. "Last night when we were here at the house someone was peeking in the window."

"What was that all about?"

"I have no idea. Hopefully I'll find out before long."

"Be careful, Crabtree," Sergeant Guthrie admonished before he hung up.

Tempe returned to the kitchen and a plate of scrambled eggs, crisp bacon, and toasted English muffins sitting on a woven place mat on a small, wooden table. "Yum, this looks good." She sat down.

Abby placed a steaming cup of coffee in front of her. "Did

you sleep well?" She set another full plate and mug on the mat opposite and sat down.

"Yes, except for crazy dreams about Big Foot chasing me through the redwoods."

Abby laughed. "You won't have to worry about that happening. Big Foot doesn't chase people."

"How about you? How was your night?"

"I had difficulty staying asleep. Kept waking up and remembering Vanessa is dead. I'm having trouble getting it through my head."

"I know. That kind of news is always hard to grasp." Tempe thought briefly about how difficult it was to believe after she learned her first husband had been killed in the line of duty. Even though it happened long ago, it still brought an ache to her heart.

For a few moments, they both ate quietly.

Abby pointed to a jar of jam. Try some of this on your muffin. It's wild blackberry. Picked the berries and put them up myself."

The jam was scrumptious and they ate in silence for awhile.

Abby picked her mug up in two hands and sipped. "Justine and I need to plan a memorial service for Vanessa. There isn't anyone else who should do it. I know she'd want to be buried here. How do I go about getting her remains?"

"I'll talk to my Sergeant and see when they can be released."

"Thank you." She put the mug back down on the table. "So what would you like to do today?"

"Can we find Jim Wyrick? You said he was still around."

Abby raised her dark eyebrows. "I know he didn't have anything to do with Vanessa's death. I doubt he even knew where she lived."

"I don't want to go back home and have the detectives ask me why I didn't interview everyone with a connection to Vanessa."

"I'll call his wife and find out where he's working so you

can talk to him away from his family."

"Good idea. I also want to stop by the sheriff's station to see if they've any information about this Lanny fellow. Do you know where he lives?"

Abby shook her head. "I haven't thought about him in years. He could be back here for all I know. I doubt if I'd even recognize him."

"Later, I'd like you to tell me everything you know about Acton Ainsworth."

Abby laughed. "I never met the guy. All I know is what Vanessa told me."

"That's exactly what I want to hear. Let me help you clean up and whatever else you need to do so we can get started. The sooner I find out everything I need to know about Vanessa, the sooner I can get back home."

∽∾

They found Jim Wyrick doing carpentry work on a new house that was going up in the middle of a grove of huge redwoods. Several big trees had been felled to clear a space for the home. Huge stumps still dotted the perimeter. After Tempe parked the car off the road, she and Abby started toward the construction site, skirting a stack of redwood planks.

Tempe stared at Abby with an unspoken question.

She returned the look. "Yes, it's ironic, isn't it? Everyone is hollering about preserving the redwoods and yet they are still being cut down to make way for buildings. The worst is Pelican Bay State Prison. They built that monstrosity right in the middle of what had once been three hundred acres of redwood forest."

Tempe knew very little about the prison except that it was purported to house the very worst offenders. She'd heard about hunger strikes and prisoners' protests, but didn't know the details. No doubt the prison brought jobs to an area that desperately needed them, but that comment was better left unsaid. Her trip to Crescent City was for one reason, to find out information about Vanessa Ainsworth that might help lead a trail to her murderer.

"Jim's over there." Abby pointed out a short, heavy-set man, obviously Native American, with a long black pony tail laced with silver strands that flowed from beneath his hard hat. He wore a sweatshirt with the sleeves cut out, showing large muscular arms. On his upper arm was a tattoo of a Native American man with the same 111 marking on his chin that Justine had on hers.

Abby waved and hollered, "Jim, have you got a minute? I've got someone here who'd like to talk to you."

Jim acknowledged her with a nod of his head. Before coming closer to the two women, he spoke briefly to a man with a huge belly, also wearing a hardhat and carrying a clipboard.

"Hey, Abby, how are you? I heard the horrible news about Vanessa." Tears glistened in his eyes. He gave them a quick swipe and peered at Tempe. "You must be the deputy who's here trying to find out stuff about Vanessa." He stuck a beefy hand toward Tempe. "Jim Wyrick. How can I help you, Deputy?"

She shook his hand and said, "Call me Tempe. Do you remember when you last saw Vanessa?"

He pulled off his hard hat and scratched his head. "Geez, I don't know. I'll have to think about that one. It was a long, long time ago is all I know." He stared off into what was left of the redwoods.

"Did you see her on her last visit? That was about three years ago," Abby prompted.

He thought some more. "You know what? I was probably in rehab then. I vaguely remember someone telling me she was around. Sorry. Back then, things were pretty foggy. All I can say is it's been years since I've seen her. She did call me once. I think after you'd told her what a mess I'd become. She scolded me. Told me things about myself I didn't really want to hear, though I knew what she said was true. Wish she was around so she could see how much I've changed." Once again his eyes glistened.

"Is there anything else about Vanessa I ought to know?"

Tempe asked.

"Have you talked to that crazy stalker guy yet? I wouldn't put anything past him," Jim said.

"Do you know if he's in town?" Abby asked.

"I thought I saw him a couple of times lately. If it was him, he's a bit heavier than he used to be, pretty much like all the rest of us. Still as weird as ever."

"What do you mean by weird?" Tempe asked.

"Oh, the guy is spooky. Wears black trench coats and hats. Walks around like a cartoon spy. Darts in and out of places. Always looking around like someone or something's after him."

"Hey, Wyrick, we need you over here," someone hollered from the building site.

"Look, I have to get back to work. If you have any more questions, call me at home. Come over if you'd like. I know my wife would like to see you again, Abby. In case you're wondering, my crush on Vanessa was over a long, long time ago."

"Thanks," Tempe said. "You've been very helpful."

"I don't know about that, but if you can think of anything else you want from me, I'll be around."

"If I do I'll give you a call," Tempe said.

As they walked back to the rental car, Abby said, "Where to now?"

"I'd like to go to the sheriff's station and see if they have any information about this Lanny guy."

While they drove toward their destination, Abby used her cell phone to dial the number Tempe had for Sergeant Glade. When he answered, she handed the phone to Tempe.

"Sergeant Glade, this is Deputy Crabtree."

"Hello, Deputy, how are you doing in our fair city?"

"It's a beautiful place. I'm on my way to the station and I wonder if I could talk to you about a fellow named Lanny Hargrove."

There was a short silence, followed by a huge sigh. "Strange guy, Hargrove. I'd like to hear why you're interested in him. I'll be waiting."

In ten minutes, they were sitting in Sergeant Glade's office. The sergeant didn't hide his displeasure at seeing Abby with Tempe, but he offered both of them a seat before settling behind his desk.

"First, what is your interest in our resident character?" he asked.

"You've just answered my first question," Tempe said.

He frowned. "What?"

"I wanted to know if he was living in Crescent City now."

"Oh. Unfortunately, yes. He was gone for awhile, but he's been back for several years and has made a nuisance of himself."

"In what way?" Tempe asked.

"Before I answer that, tell me why you're asking about him."

"Abigail told me that Lanny stalked Vanessa Ainsworth when they were in high school and continued when Vanessa went to UCSB. He didn't stop even after she graduated and began working. Isn't that right, Abby?"

"Yes. Vanessa complained about him all the time."

"Did she ever make a formal complaint to law enforcement?"

Abby shook her head. "Not while she lived here. When it continued in Santa Barbara, at her fiancé's urging, she finally did it."

"When did it stop, if it did?" Sheriff Glade asked.

"When she got married, I suppose. I don't really know. We weren't in touch much after that."

Tempe thought for a moment. "What I'm wondering is if Lanny managed to find her in Bear Creek. If he did, perhaps Vanessa did something to make him angry enough to kill her."

Abby raised her eyebrows.

The sheriff cocked his head and pursed his lips. "Hmmm. That's an interesting theory. When was the victim killed?"

Tempe told him the approximate date of Vanessa's murder.

He opened a drawer in his desk, pulled out a file folder

and scanned it. "We didn't have any calls about him during that period, so I suppose it's a possibility."

This information piqued Tempe's curiosity. "What kind of calls do you usually get about him?"

"He's a pest. Harmless, really. At least that's what we've always thought. He discovers conspiracies all over the place. He thinks every dark skinned man around, who isn't Indian or Mexican, is probably a terrorist. He spies on them long enough for the person to get suspicious and call us about a stranger lurking around his store or home. It's unbelievable the outlandish plots Lanny's thought up about these people. For an example, he decided one of the local physicians, an Indian from India, was planning to set bombs during the Aleutian Goose Festival. Crazy. He made an absolute nuisance of himself, following the doc around, peeking in his windows at his office and at home. We brought Lanny in, gave him a lecture and threatened him with jail time." Sergeant Glade drummed a pencil against his desk. "What the man needs is a mental institution."

"I'd like to talk to him. Do you have his address?"

The sergeant sighed. "Now that one is a problem. I don't think he has a permanent address."

"He's homeless?" Tempe asked.

"Not exactly. He has an old VW camper bus. He lives in that mostly. Stays at campgrounds where he can get away without paying. We've had lots of complaints about that. He's been chased away from viewpoints and rest stops. His favorite hangouts lately seem to be in people's yards."

"Do you have a list of his friends where he might stay?" Tempe asked.

"Well, you see, it isn't friends' yards where he stays. He just finds a place where he won't be noticed. Often he isn't. There's lots of open space around here. When he is spotted, the people order him away. Some call us. He's just one of several wackos we put up with." He stared at Abby for a moment.

"What does this guy live on?"

"I'm not sure. There are lots of rumors. He received an

inheritance that comes in monthly. He might get some sort of disability for not being quite right in the head. In either case, he probably picks up his mail General Delivery at the post office."

For the first time, Abby spoke. "I think your first supposition is right. As I remember, when we were in school his folks were pretty well off. Lived in a great big house on a bluff overlooking the ocean. They were a bit on the eccentric side too and kept to themselves. I can't remember the dates, but sometime while he was off to school his parents died in an accident."

Sergeant Glade's expression displayed something Tempe couldn't quite read. Was it disbelief, or perhaps disgust? In any case, he'd made it obvious that he certainly didn't like Abby.

He nodded. "Hmmm. Never heard that one before."

Abby raised an eyebrow in Tempe's direction, crossed her arms and settled back in her chair.

"Do you have any other information that might help me?" Tempe asked.

The sergeant glanced at the watch on his wrist. "Nope. Can't think of a thing."

"You might be interested to know we had a Peeping Tom at Abby's last night. I think it might have something to do with this case," Tempe said.

Sergeant Glade stared at Abby for a long moment. "Oh, I doubt that. Ms. Jacoby has created lots of enemies in the last few years. It was someone whose toes she's stepped on during one of her many protests." He rose from his chair. "Now, if that's all, I have some important business to tend to."

Tempe stood and offered her hand to the sergeant. "I just wanted you to know in case something happens. If we should need your assistance, your offer to help is still good, isn't it?"

The Sergeant's tanned face colored. He shook her hand but quickly released it. "Of course you can expect assistance from one of my deputies, as long as you're not calling about some nonsense."

As Tempe and Abby left, Abby turned back long enough to smile and say, "Nice to see you again, Sergeant Glade."

He didn't respond.

Once back inside the rental car, Tempe turned to Abby. "You're not one of his favorite people."

She laughed. "Certainly looks that way, doesn't it? We didn't find out anything helpful, did we?"

"Actually, we did. We were tailed all the way here by an old VW camper."

Turning around to look over her shoulder, she asked, "We were? I didn't notice."

"He's very good at what he does. Most lay people who try to follow someone are so obvious they are noticed right away. Lanny, if that's who it is in the VW camper, has stayed three or four cars back. I don't see him right now, but I bet as soon as we get back into traffic, he'll be right there again."

# CHAPTER 11

"What are we going to do about this guy?" Abby asked. "I can't imagine why he'd want to keep following us."

"I think we ought to confront him." Tempe kept glancing in her mirrors. It wasn't long before she spotted the old blue-and-white bus about three cars back.

"Is that a good idea?"

"I'd like to know what he thinks he's doing. Has he ever been a physical threat to anyone?"

"No, not really. He just was a big pest to Vanessa. She couldn't go anywhere or do anything that he didn't pop up. Like I said, it ended after she got married. Or at least I think it did. I didn't hear from her for awhile after she married Acton. Then when I did, she only told me how bad the marriage had become. What a different guy Acton turned out to be than what she'd thought."

"I want to hear more about him and the marriage, but right now, let's concentrate on Lanny, or whoever is driving that VW bus."

"What are you going to do?"

"No doubt he was the one Justine caught peeking in the windows at us. Why don't we head back to your place and see if he follows us? He has no idea we're on to him. We can go inside, then I'll sneak out the back and see if I can catch him."

Tempe drove directly back to Abby's house, parked the car, and both women went inside. "Do whatever you would ordinarily. I'll see if our shadow is lurking around somewhere."

"Be careful," Abby said.

Tempe slipped out the back door. For a moment, she stood quietly, breathing in the wonderful scent from the redwoods surrounding Abby's house. Moving from thick tree trunk to tree trunk, Tempe made her way toward the road. Keeping herself concealed, she moved close enough to see any vehicles that might be parked along the way.

Abby's neighborhood was sparsely settled, with small, old houses, many of them not much more than cabins, others single-wide mobile homes. All of them were set back, many hidden from view by the thick growth of redwoods and pines. Instead of weeds, huge ferns filled the open places. Smoke came from some chimneys, testifying to a few residents being at home. Tempe hoped no one would spot her skulking around and call the sheriff's department. That would be humiliating.

She passed by three homes, some with old vehicles parked in dirt driveways, before she spotted the VW. It was tucked in back of a large stake truck filled with firewood. Tempe maneuvered herself behind the bus. From where she squatted near the back bumper, she could see the back of the driver's head.

*Here goes nothing.* Taking her revolver out of the holster, she sprang to her feet, leaped toward the driver's door and yanked it open.

A man with brown curly hair, a wide forehead, and small dark eyes that nearly popped with surprise, turned toward her. "What the heck? Who are you? Is that a gun?"

Tempe reached in and pulled his keys from the ignition. "Don't you know? You've been following me around all morning."

"Hey, give me my keys. What do you think you're doing?" He grabbed for her hand, but she'd already pocketed the keys.

"I'll give them back to you as soon as I find out why you've been following me around."

He blinked and then squinted at her. "I don't know who you are."

"Maybe not, but you do know who Abigail Jacoby is, don't you?"

His long, thin face paled. "What business is it of yours?"

"For your information, Mr. Hargrove, I'm a deputy sheriff from Tulare County."

Lanny, if that's who he was, asked, "How did you know who I am?"

"Oh, I've heard a lot about you. How you like to stalk people, people like Vanessa Ainsworth."

His voice rose nearly an octave. "I didn't stalk Vanessa."

"According to the sheriff in Crescent City and Vanessa's cousin Abigail, you certainly did."

"That's what they called it, but I was in love with Vanessa. If she'd given me a chance, she'd have grown to love me back."

He was either extremely clever, or he didn't know about Vanessa's murder. "Lanny, why don't we walk up to Abigail's house? I have something I need to talk to you about."

He frowned. "What possible interest could you have in me?"

"For starters, I want to know why you've been following me and Abigail. Now, come on, get out of the bus. It's the only way you're getting your keys back." Tempe lowered the revolver and stepped back from the VW.

Obviously reluctant, Lanny opened the door and stepped down. He was at least six feet tall, and the long, black trench coat he wore made him look bigger than he was. When the door swung open, Tempe could see he was slender. His black turtleneck sweater hugged his narrow frame. Long thin legs were encased in black slacks and he wore polished black boots.

"Come on," Tempe said, "Abigail's place is only a little way up the hill. I'm sure you're already familiar with where she lives. You were peeking in her window the other night, weren't you." The last she said was a statement, not a question.

He'd been keeping pace beside her, but he halted at that last remark. "I don't know what you're talking about. I never peeked in her window or anyone else's."

Because she was afraid he'd change his mind about going with her if she pursued the subject, Tempe said, "Okay. I guess it wasn't you."

When they reached the house, Abby opened the front door as they approached. Lanny stepped behind Tempe as though he feared Abby—or perhaps he was ashamed at being caught following her.

Abby frowned at the gun in Tempe's hand.

Feeling sure she wouldn't have any trouble from Lanny, Tempe holstered it.

"Hello, Lanny. It's been a long time since I've seen you." Abby smiled at him and opened the door wider. "Come in."

Tempe gestured for Lanny to enter and she followed.

He remained standing until Tempe sat on the couch and Abby sat in her usual spot in the wooden chair with all the pillows. Lanny sat as far away from Abby as possible, on a straight- backed chair on the other side of the room.

"Now, that we're all here together, Lanny tell us why you were tailing us," Tempe said.

He hung his head as though ashamed. "I wanted to find out if you knew anything about Vanessa. Where she's living now, what she's doing."

"If you wanted to know that, why didn't you just come to the door and ask me?" Abby asked.

"I didn't think you'd talk to me," he said.

"How would following Abby change that?" Tempe asked.

"I don't know. I just thought maybe that she might go some place where she would feel comfortable enough to talk to me."

"If that was so, why didn't you approach her in the casino when you were spying on us there?"

Once again, his small eyes widened. "I wasn't spying on you at any casino."

Tempe said. "Are you telling me it wasn't you?"

He shook his head so hard, his curls bounced. "That's right, it wasn't me."

If he was telling the truth, that meant there was someone

else watching Tempe and Abby. If so, who could it be and why? Tempe decided Lanny just didn't want to admit what he'd been up to.

"Lanny, there's something we need to tell you. Something you haven't heard yet."

He frowned. "What?"

"It's bad news about Vanessa," Abby said, tears brimming her eyes.

"What is it? Is Vanessa sick? Was she in an accident?" He glanced quickly from Abby to Tempe. "Please."

Abby shook her head. She plucked a tissue from a pocket in her skirt and wiped her eyes.

It was up to Tempe to finish breaking the bad news. "Lanny, I hate to be the one to tell you this. It's obvious you cared for Vanessa." She paused.

Leaning forward, Lanny frowned.

There was no easy way to do it. "Vanessa was murdered."

"Oh, my God, it can't be true!"

"I'm afraid it is, Lanny. I saw her body."

He leaped to his feet. "Are you sure? Who did it?"

"We don't know. That's one of the reasons I'm here, to see if I can find out something that might help with the investigation," Tempe said.

Lanny blinked. At first Tempe thought he was going to cry, but instead he shouted, "Oh, no. You came here because you thought I might be the killer." He backed into his chair and sat down heavily.

"No, that's not true," Tempe said. "I was sent up here to find out all I could about Vanessa and everyone who knew her. You're only one of several people who have been mentioned. I must tell you though, your actions have made me wonder about you."

"What do you mean, my actions?" he asked.

"Following us around. That isn't something an innocent person does."

"I told you, I just wanted to find out about Vanessa." The fact that she was dead must've finally struck Lanny. His face seemed to crumble. His body shook with sobs. He buried his face in his hands.

Abby began to cry too. Through her tears, she said, "We'll all miss her."

Tempe stood. It was clear that Lanny had no previous knowledge of Vanessa's death. Though probably unbalanced, his reactions convinced Tempe he wasn't a suspect. She fished his keys from her pocket. She patted his shoulder and offered the keys. "Here, take them. I'm sorry I had to be the one to deliver the bad news."

Lanny lifted his tear-streaked face. "Where is the funeral going to be? I'd really like to be there."

"We'll have a memorial service for her," Abby said. "Once I've made the plans I'll put something in the paper."

After pocketing the keys, Lanny said, "Could I call you later? Find out the details?"

"Sure, that'll be fine," Abby said.

Turning to Tempe, Lanny said, "I don't remember your name."

Tempe put out her hand. "I'm Deputy Tempe Crabtree."

He clasped it briefly. "Is it okay if I go now? I've got to think about this. I haven't seen Vanessa for so long." He sniffed and brushed a tear away with his hand. "Now I never will again."

"Yes, you can leave, but promise me, if you want to know anything else, how about just approaching me or Abby? No more of this tailing folks."

He nodded. "I guess I was pretty stupid."

"Actually, you did a pretty good job of it."

He smiled briefly. He sniffed a couple of times, opened the door and disappeared. In a few minutes, Tempe heard the unmistakable sputtering of the VW bus starting up.

"What was with the gun?" Abby said.

"I've been carrying the whole time I've been here. I am a deputy on assignment, after all. I had no idea whether or not Lanny was armed."

"I'm not against guns, but I was surprised to see yours.

My rifle is locked up in my bedroom closet." She thought for a moment. "So what do you think about Lanny?"

"He's a strange fellow, but I don't think he had anything to do with Vanessa's death," Tempe said.

"What are you going to do now?"

"I don't think there's anything I can find out here that will help the investigation."

"I'm sorry we haven't been more helpful," Abby said.

"You couldn't have been more hospitable. I appreciate all you've done for me. I guess I'll call my boss and let him know that this was a futile trip. Do you mind if I use your phone?"

Before Abby could answer, the telephone rang.

# CHAPTER 12

When Abby hung up the phone, she turned to Tempe and said, "That was Justine. She'd like us to come to the tea house this evening for a special event."

"Once I call my sergeant and tell him this was a big waste of time, he's going to insist I catch the next plane home."

"Don't call him yet. You might find this interesting."

Curious, Tempe agreed. "Perhaps one of you will remember something about Vanessa that could shed some light on who might have killed her and why. I have a hunch it's not going to be anyone from around here."

"You're probably right. I've been trying to remember if there's anything about Vanessa that I haven't told you."

"What about her life after she married Acton Ainsworth? Did she tell you about that period of her life?"

"I thought he had an alibi for the time that Vanessa was murdered," Abby said.

"That's what I was told, but I don't know what else I can find out while I'm here except what you know about Vanessa's marriage. Maybe what you remember will lead me somewhere else. I'd like to have something to go back and tell my Sergeant. The department spent a lot of money to fly me here." Tempe smiled. "And if it hadn't been for you and your hospitality, it would have been a lot more."

"I've enjoyed having you here, but I wouldn't be much of a hostess if I didn't offer you lunch. I don't know about you, but I'm getting hungry. How about a bowl of soup?"

"Don't go to too much trouble," Tempe said. "I'd be happy with a piece of bread and more of that wonderful blackberry jam."

"It won't be any trouble, I'll just open a can. You most certainly can have some more of my jam. Come on in the kitchen with me and I'll tell you all I can remember about Acton and Vanessa's marriage."

While the chicken noodle soup heated, Abby brought out the bread and jam and sorted through her memories about the time Vanessa spent with Acton. "I only know bits and pieces. The marriage wasn't very old when Vanessa found out that Acton was extremely jealous. So jealous that he didn't want her to have friends of her own. I hadn't heard from her for a long while, a couple of years, actually, then one night she called me collect. I could tell she was upset. Soon as she asked about everyone around here she started crying. When I asked her what was wrong, she said, 'I made a big mistake. Acton isn't the man I thought he was. He won't let me do anything.' I asked her if he kept her from painting. She said, 'No, but that's the only thing he lets me do. The reason I haven't called is because he won't let me use the phone.'

"She went on to tell me that the only reason she was calling then was because Acton was on a furniture buying trip and she'd walked a mile from their home to a gas station to use a pay phone. He encouraged her to paint but wouldn't allow her to show her paintings because then she'd be out of the house. He didn't want her to talk to anyone or go anywhere unless it was with him." Abby poured the hot soup into two bowls and brought them to the table.

"Did she say anything about him being physically abusive?" Tempe asked. She scooped some soup on her spoon and blew on it.

"Not then. What was going on sounded more like psychological abuse. The whole thing was kind of ironic because Vanessa always said she'd never marry an Indian because so many of them abused their wives. That was something she swore she'd never tolerate."

For a few moments, Tempe ate her soup and thought about what Abby told her before responding. "How long was Vanessa married to Ainsworth before she left him?"

"Far longer than I ever expected. From what she told me, she'd threaten to divorce him, and then he'd promise not to be so paranoid. He let her show her paintings in some of the galleries around Santa Barbara and even farther up the coast in places like Carmel."

Tempe thought about what Abby said. "You used a word I hadn't heard in connection with Vanessa's husband before."

Abby frowned. "What word?"

"Paranoid. How was he paranoid?"

"I'll have to think about that. I know that's what Vanessa called him. He always thought someone was out to do him in, especially in the business world. In Vanessa's case, he thought if she left him, it would be to take him for all he was worth. In the end, she did get plenty from him, but he deserved to pay after making her life miserable for so long."

"I suppose a lot of men with money might feel like that." Tempe slathered blackberry jam on a piece of bread. "This is absolutely wonderful. I've never done any canning."

"I learned way back when I was a kid. Blackberries grow wild around here. My mother preserved everything. My father had odd jobs. People didn't hire Indians for work that paid much money. Of course he fished and hunted when he could to add to our food supply. Mom had yard sales to make ends meet."

"What kind of jobs are available to the Indians now?" Tempe licked jam off her finger.

"Of course there are the casinos and some have jobs at the prison. Those require clean records. Some work on the lily bulb farms or the fish plants. Unfortunately, a lot of our women live with abusive men, or their men are in prison. They have a bunch of kids and get welfare. Too many are in the lost soul's paradise, using alcohol and drugs." Abby sighed.

"We have some of those same problems at home. Though I must say the casino has helped the people on the Bear Creek reservation. Now there are more jobs and they don't have to go so far to find work."

Abby's laugh was far from amused. "The casinos have helped in some ways and caused problems in others. Indians gamble too and often when they shouldn't. That's one reason Justine boycotts them. Another is that too many Tolowa have completely forgotten their heritage and have become more interested in their new SUVs, big trucks and other toys."

Talk like this always made Tempe feel guilty. Though she knew more than she had a few years ago, thanks to Nick Two John and other Indian friends, her ancestry had never been in the forefront of her life. She didn't even know much about the history of the Yanduchi Indians. Hutch discouraged her from taking part in the spiritual side, though at times she did anyway, but she'd made no real effort to understand what it meant to be a Native American.

Abby and Justine's passion about keeping the old ways alive made Tempe uncomfortable. Was it really important that people remember what had gone on before? Tempe had enough trouble taking care of what happened in her day-to-day life. Right now, she needed to concentrate on learning about Vanessa Ainsworth and trying to discover some information that might be useful to take back to the detectives.

Picking up her bowl and spoon, Tempe put them in the sink. "Thank you, Abby, that really hit the spot. Is there something I can do to help you this afternoon?"

"Actually there is. If you don't mind, you could drive me around while I pick up a few things for tonight. I need to go to the bank, and if I don't pay my electric bill, they may turn off my lights."

"Sure, I'll be glad to." Before they left, Tempe put on her shoulder holster with her gun, hiding it under her turquoise jacket. *Who was being paranoid now?*

After a couple of stops, Tempe noticed that somebody was following again, only this time it wasn't in a Volkswagen bus.

# CHAPTER 13

By the time Tempe had driven Abby into Crescent City to the bank and to a market where she paid her electric bill, Tempe knew for certain they were being followed by a black sedan. This tail was even better than Lanny's. Their new shadow stayed several cars back. Sometimes he passed them and continued as though it was only a coincidence that he kept appearing.

When he did pass, Tempe saw the driver of the sedan was a clean-shaven, white male wearing a baseball cap. She'd never seen him before.

One of Abby's last errands was to visit a deli. Tempe waited in the car and watched the black sedan cruise slowly by and turn at the next corner. Watching in the side mirror, Tempe wasn't the least bit surprised when she spotted the same car pulling into a parking spot at the end of the block.

Abby came out of the deli carrying a large box. Tempe jumped from the rental car and opened the back door for her. Once Abby had deposited her purchase and slid into the passenger seat, Tempe settled in beside her, but didn't start the car.

With a question in her voice, Abby said, "Something's going on."

"We've got another shadow," Tempe said. "Take a peek. It's the black sedan in back of us, parked near the corner."

Abby raised up and peered in the rearview mirror as if to check her makeup. "Oh, I see it. Are you sure it's following us?"

"Oh yes. I spotted the car soon after we left your place. Didn't think too much about it though, until we got to the bank. He pulled into the parking lot but never got out. When we left, so did he." Tempe turned the key in the ignition. "Where to now?"

Abby pointed over her shoulder. "Let's go to the galleria. I got the sandwiches for later. We can give Justine a hand getting ready."

"What's happening tonight?" Tempe asked.

"Story telling. You might find it entertaining."

Tempe watched the traffic. When there was an opening, she drove away from the curb. "Watch. He'll let a few cars go by and then he'll come after us. Just for fun, I think I'll forget to turn on my signal and make a quick right at the next corner."

Their tail missed the turn, but was back in place before they'd gone two blocks.

Abby, who'd been watching in her side mirror said, "He's back."

"I could lose him, but it wouldn't do much good since whoever it is knows where you live and this place isn't large enough for anyone to disappear."

"Do you think it's Lanny again?"

"No, I'm sure it isn't. I think Lanny was truthful in telling us that he was following us to find out if we knew anything about Vanessa. Once he learned she was dead, that was it. I'm sure he's holed up somewhere, mourning."

"You're probably right. Nearly his whole life he's been fixated on Vanessa. He probably feels like he's lost a part of himself."

"I'd like to know who this new person is and whether he's tailing me or you."

Abby gasped, "Why on earth would anyone be tailing me?"

"It's just a thought, but I wondered if it might be someone from the sheriff's department. If it is, maybe they want to keep an eye on you. They seem to take an unusual interest in your activities."

"I don't think they are all that interested in me. Oh sure, they'd like to catch me doing something illegal, but they never will because all I'm interested in is making things better for the Tolowa and making sure our people don't forget who they are and where they came from."

"It's obvious Sergeant Glade isn't exactly crazy about you."

"It isn't just me. It's Indians in general. He, along with a lot of other folks, would be much happier if we'd just disappear. It really isn't much different than the old days."

Tempe considered this she drove along the scenic highway toward the galleria.

"If it isn't the sheriff's department who put a tail on us, who could it be?"

"I don't have an answer. How're you going to find out?"

"It won't be as easy to confront whoever it is as it was Lanny, now that he knows we're on to him. We'll go about our business. An opportunity will present itself, I'm sure." Tempe turned the car into the road that led to the galleria.

❦

By six o'clock, Tempe, Abby and Justine had readied the galleria for the expected guests. The sandwiches Abby had picked up at the deli were arranged on platters and set out on a long table alongside dips and chips, and a variety of homemade cookies. A selection of herbal teas, honey, paper plates and cups were set on the counter beside a coffee pot filled with hot water. Soft drinks and bottled water poked through an ice-filled chest at the end of the table.

Justine wore a beaded vest over a simple, ankle length denim dress. She glanced at her watch. "People will start showing up any minute now. What have you two been up to all day?"

"I told Tempe about Vanessa's marriage and how Acton treated her," Abby said.

"We might as well sit." Justine pointed toward chairs and

benches arranged around the redwood walls. Once they were seated, she added, "Poor Vanessa, left home to avoid being married to an Indian who might abuse her and she ended up with someone far worse. Why she stayed with him as long as she did, I don't know."

"Because she had a hard time getting away from him," Abby said.

"Did either of you ever meet him?" Tempe asked.

Justine snorted. "Are you kidding? He wasn't about to let any of her old friends visit. He sure didn't want any of his cronies to find out Vanessa was an Indian. And he wouldn't let her come to Crescent City. I don't think he allowed her to go anywhere by herself. Even when she had a gallery showing, he dogged her steps. He didn't want her being by herself with any of the gallery owners."

"I think the detectives will find all this interesting. They sure need to recheck Ainsworth's alibi."

Abby told Justine about Lanny and what happened with him and finished with, "Now we've got someone else following us. Came all the way here, but went on up the road. No reason for him to go farther unless he lives up there or is visiting someone."

Before Justine could comment, the first group of people burst into the room, greeting Abby and Justine loudly, along with big hugs. The room filled quickly. Tempe was introduced to everyone and they welcomed her warmly. Family groups with small children helped themselves to the food and conversations buzzed. Older people arrived, some who were obviously Indians, others who weren't.

Once most of the food was eaten, and people settled in chairs or benches with their favorite hot beverage or punch, Justine called for quiet. "Let's begin with our favorite story. Ben, will you tell it, please?"

Ben, a Tolowa with a dark, deeply lined face, sat at the end of the room. Silver braids interlaced with colorful ribbons draped over the shoulders of his worn, denim shirt. The younger children gathered at his feet. He began his story with,

"Long, long ago came a great rain. It rained and rained and rained. The water rose higher and higher. All the valleys became lakes. The people ran up into the mountains. But the water kept coming. The people went as far and as high as they could, but the water kept rising. All the people were swept away and drowned." He paused, and the children gasped.

"All but one man and one woman who reached the highest peak of the mountain and they were saved. These Indians ate fish from the water that was around them.

"Finally the water went down. The animals were gone. The dead children of these two Indians became the spirits of the deer and the bear. Then all the animals and insects came back to earth again.

"But the Indians didn't have fire. The big flood had put out all the fires everywhere. They looked at the moon and wished they could get fire from it. The Spider Indians and the Snake Indians put their heads together and came up with a plan to steal fire. The Spider Indians wove a light balloon and fastened it by a long rope to the earth. They climbed into the balloon and started for the moon. When they got there, the Indians who lived on the moon were suspicious of the Indians who came from earth. But the Spider Indians said, 'We just came here to gamble.' The Moon Indians believed them and they all sat by the fire and making bets and throwing stones.

"The Snake Indians sent a man to climb the long rope from the earth to the moon. When he reached the top, before the Moon Indians realized what he was up to, he ran through the fire and stole it. He slid down the rope to the earth. Once he reached the earth he traveled over the rocks, the trees and the dry sticks and gave the fire to each. Everything he touched contained fire. So the world became bright again, as it was before the flood.

"When the Spider Indians returned to earth, the other Indians killed them so the Moon Indians wouldn't seek revenge."

Tempe wasn't sure what the moral of the story was, or if there was one, but she had heard that every culture had a flood story, and she knew the Yanduchi had one of their own.

A wizened old woman who sat next to the first story teller told a wistful tale about a flying tortoise.

More stories followed. A handsome younger man whose Indian heritage wasn't as obvious as most of the others told about the Aleutian geese. "Too many were killed by hunters for sport and they nearly disappeared from our skies, but now they are a returning to us. The geese are part of the Tolowa creation story. Every spring the sound of geese is everywhere. The Tolowa word for geese is '*Haa-chu*'. *Haa* is the sound of the honking of the geese and *–chu* means a lot or big. When you hear these geese you know spring is on the way."

A middle-aged woman began a story with, "Deep in the forest live big creatures who are hairy all over. There are those who say these creatures aren't real, but I am here to tell you that they are."

The children gasped. Justine jabbed Tempe in the side with her elbow and whispered. "See, I told you Bigfoot is real."

The children's eyes grew bigger and they drew closer to the woman as she spoke.

"These stories have been passed down from one generation to another. My great-great grandfather said when he was a boy and was hunting, he knew he was being followed. He hid behind a bush and saw a tall, muscular creature covered with hair, standing behind a tree. When he told his father, his father said, "These are the people who share the bounty of the forests and the rivers and the sea with the Indians. They have never harmed the Indians.

"Another of my relatives saw a mother with her child. The young one was playing near a creek when she noticed the Indians. She grabbed the youngster and pulled him in front of her, taking him back through the trees. Both of them were covered in fur."

She told of other encounters with the large, hairy creatures. Sometimes people knew they were near because of their rancid smell. Sometimes they would steal the Indians' food, but they never harmed anyone.

Other stories about Big Foot sightings were told, followed by more Indian legends. The story telling lasted far into the night. About the time Tempe wondered if the event would ever end, people began gathering up their children and their belongings, saying their goodnights and leaving.

"Well, what did you think?" Justine asked Tempe, as they and Abby tackled the clean-up.

"It was fun. I've never been to anything like this before," Tempe said.

"Really?" Justine sounded incredulous. "Don't they have story telling on the Bear Creek reservation?"

"Perhaps they do, but I've never heard about it. But a lot goes on there that I'm not aware of." Like Nick Two John, Justine had a way of making Tempe feeling guilty because she lacked knowledge of her Indian heritage. "I don't live on the reservation. I'm married to a preacher, have a college-age son, and being a deputy takes up a lot of my time."

Justine paused from dumping a small waste paper basket into a larger trash can. "You're married to a preacher? A Christian preacher?"

# CHAPTER 14

"That's right," Tempe said. "He's the pastor of the Bear Creek Community Church."

"That must be fun," Justine said, not smiling.

Abby quirked an eyebrow in Tempe's direction. "Justine doesn't like Christians much."

"It's not that I don't like them," Justine protested, "but they shouldn't try to make the people abandon our religion to become Christians."

"I've met folks on our rez who have made a nice compromise between the two," Tempe said.

That Justine didn't think much of that idea either was evidenced by the rude sound she made with her mouth.

"Be fair, Justine," Abby said, "isn't that more or less what the Shaker church was, a compromise? After all, the Shakers drew on the traditional Indian belief that everything is surrounded by God and influenced by God. Believers follow the Gospel of Jesus Christ though some don't believe in the Bible. Instead they believe that the essence of the gospel message is written in a person's subconscious."

Justine nodded, "Something like that. But they also had healings and sometimes fell into trances."

"It isn't any of my business, but I'm curious, Tempe, what are you?" Abby asked.

Tempe frowned. "What do you mean?"

"What's your religion?"

"Mostly Christian, but I've got to admit I've dabbled a bit

in some native spiritualism," Tempe said. "Didn't make my husband very happy."

"I guess not," Justine said. "What kind of spiritualism?"

"Once I participated in a grieving ceremony. Another time, I called someone back from the dead," Tempe said.

"Really? Maybe you're more of an Indian than I gave you credit for," Justine said. "Too bad you won't be here for Vanessa's mourning ceremony."

"I wish I could, but I'm planning to leave tomorrow." Tempe glanced around at the disarray. "Do you want us to rearrange the chairs?"

Justine glanced around. "No, they're fine. Why don't we have another cup of coffee before I lock up?"

"Sounds good to me." Abby pulled chairs up to the table and Justine brought over the coffee pot.

Tempe enjoyed these two women even though her visit hadn't provided the answers the detectives had hoped for. "Since I can't be here, tell me about the ceremony you'll have for Vanessa."

"Nothing like in the old days. When I was young, the dead were usually kept at home in a simple coffin for several days. Everyone came to view the body and cried and wailed. By the time the body was taken to the Shaker Church, it didn't look so good. All I remember was the Bible, bells and candles and lots of chanting and singing. Everyone moved counter-clockwise around the room. People put things in with the body."

"What kind of things?" Tempe asked.

"Oh, beads, bits of ribbon, pretty rocks," Justine said.

Abby giggled. "Tell about what you put into the coffin at your aunt's funeral."

Grinning, Justine said, "My dear old auntie had been a pillar of the Presbyterian church she belonged to down in Southern California. Those nice white Presbyterians were a bit shocked when my auntie's Indian relatives arrived. No one said anything when we passed by to view her body and added our tokens to the coffin. I didn't have anything, but I took a piece of gum I'd been chewing and wrapped it in foil. I stuck it under the sleeve of her pretty dress."

Tempe laughed. "That must have been something to see. I bet the white relatives had a hard time not saying anything to you."

Justine made a face. "They probably took all that stuff out and threw it away after we left. But I doubt if they knew about the gum."

"Whatever we do for Vanessa will be a bit more digni-fied. After all, she wasn't into anything Indian," Abby said, glancing at her watch. "I suspect it's about time we headed home."

Tempe stood, but before she could move there was a loud bang against the door, and heavy footsteps pounded across the wooden porch and down the steps.

"What the heck was that?" Justine cried as she leaped to her feet and headed toward the door.

# CHAPTER 15

Tempe moved right behind her. "I suspect that's our latest shadow."

Justine halted so abruptly, Tempe almost ran into her.

"Oh, yeah, who do you think it is?"

"I don't know, but if we hurry, maybe we can find out." Justine flung open the door.

Tempe pushed past her and galloped down the stairs. The other two women followed.

Looking up the hill, she saw a dark figure running. Tempe took after him, but before she narrowed the space between them, the man jumped into the same dark sedan that had been following them, fired up the engine and spun his tires as he sped off down the road.

"Too late. Did he look familiar to either of you?" Tempe asked.

"I couldn't see enough to tell," Abby said.

"Bet it's a deputy," Justine said. "They figure we're up to something."

"That's what I thought," Abby said.

Tempe shook her head. She knew the women didn't even consider the fact that she was a deputy sheriff. "I don't think so. I have a hunch it's something else entirely. Something to do with Vanessa's murder, no doubt."

"Too bad you couldn't catch him." Justine headed back up the stairs, turned off all the lights except the one over the porch, pulled the front door shut and locked it.

"Oh, he'll turn up again. I'm positive of that."

"It'll have to be pretty soon since you're planning to leave tomorrow."

"If we keep our ears open, I bet he'll make another appearance later tonight. With any luck, I'll be able to catch him then," Tempe said.

Justine put her arms around Tempe and hugged her tight. "I don't expect I'll see you tomorrow. It's been a pleasure. Hope you've enjoyed your visit with us Tolowa."

"I've loved every minute of it. I've certainly learned a lot to share with my husband. Maybe you can visit us sometime. We have an empty bedroom now that my son's at college. The invitation is open to you both. We'd love to have you. I can introduce you to some of my Yanduchi friends."

✺✺

The ride home was uneventful. No telltale headlights indicated their shadow was following. Abby obviously noting how often Tempe checked her mirrors asked, "Is he back there?"

"Not that I can detect. But he knows where you live and knows we'll be heading back home soon. He doesn't need to follow us, he'll probably be there waiting."

No obvious signs showed that anyone lurked around Abby's home, nor were there any dark sedans parked on the road either before they reached their destination, nor beyond as far as they could see in the dark. Fog roiled in and around the thick trunks of the redwood trees and obscured the view of the night sky. The heady scent of the surrounding redwoods and wood smoke filled the air. Perfect night for someone up to no good to skulk around without being noticed.

Tempe shivered.

"It is a bit cold. Once we get inside I'll build a fire," Abby said.

Tempe didn't tell her that the shivers weren't due to the chill in the air. She had the definite feeling they were being watched. Glancing around, she nothing but the fog that grew even thicker.

Despite the fire that Abby soon had crackling in the fireplace, the creepy feeling persisted inside the house.

"Only turn on a light in the kitchen," Tempe suggested. "We can see enough from there and the glow from the fire."

Abby settled herself in her usual spot and stared at Tempe. "What do you expect to happen?"

"I'm not sure, but whoever has been following isn't going to give up this easily. I have a hunch this person knows I'll be leaving soon, so whatever he's after, he's going to have to make a move pretty soon."

"So what you mean is you expect him to make a visit to the house sometime tonight."

"Yes, that's exactly what I expect. If the room isn't too well lit, maybe we'll be able to spot him if he decides to peek in the windows."

"That's what you think he'll do, spy on us?"

"For a start, at least. I don't want to scare you, but I'm getting the nasty feeling that things may get a little more exciting than that."

Abby frowned. "Do you think he wants to harm you...or me?"

"I hope not, but I don't know what he wants. We're just going to have to wait and see what happens."

≈≈

Nothing was left in the fireplace but ruby coals. Abby and Tempe had run out of topics to discuss. Tempe knew more about Abby now than she did about most of the people in Bear Creek. Deciding nothing was going to happen, Tempe started to rise.

Before she was fully in a standing position, a loud creak sounded on the porch. Tempe put a finger to her lips, but it was obvious Abby had heard it too as she slid quietly from her chair and tiptoed toward the front window. Standing to the side, she stared through the open curtains. Nodding her head, she pointed at the door.

Tempe moved silently until she had her hand on the door-knob. She paused only a moment before yanking the door open.

A man Tempe had never seen before, visibly shaken by her sudden action, stood next to the door as though he'd been listening. Partially bald with a bushy mustache, wearing a black leather jacket and jeans, the man stared directly at her with his mouth hanging open.

Before Tempe could say anything, the man bolted.

"Call 911," Tempe shouted to Abby as she took off after him, unsnapping her holster as she ran.

The man headed up the hill toward the redwood forest. While he ran on the road, it was easy enough for Tempe to follow closely behind.

With an extra burst of energy, he galloped across the street, darted into a thick grove of redwoods and disappeared.

"Darn!"

While jogging toward the place that swallowed up her quarry, Tempe wondered who she was chasing. He didn't look like the person who had been following them. Of course, the first man had worn a baseball cap, but she didn't remember a mustache. If he wasn't the driver of the black sedan, then who was he? If he was just someone coming to the door, why did he run?

Whoever he was, Tempe was determined to catch him and find out.

Once she entered the forest she realized how difficult it would be to catch up with the man, or even figure out which way he'd gone. Trapped by the big trunks of the giant red-wood and the smaller pine trees, the fog swirled thickly making it impossible to see more than a few feet ahead.

Tempe paused, listening. The floor of the forest was thickly carpeted with ferns and decaying cones dropped from the huge trees. It wouldn't be easy to hear the man's progress. Despite that, Tempe took what she thought must have been his path, the only obvious trail that wound upward through the ancient growth. She couldn't hear her prey's progress, but that meant he couldn't hear hers either.

No longer able to run, because it was so dark, Tempe concentrated on where to step. The thick fog intensified the pleasing scent of the redwoods. She continued forward, placing her feet carefully. It wouldn't do to stumble and fall. How she wished she had a flashlight as well as her gun.

After nearly fifteen minutes of the uphill climb, Tempe felt winded and thought her pursuit futile. The man might have circled around and left the forest.

She smelled something odd. The thought of coming upon Big Foot tickled her, but she quickly dismissed it when she recognized the scent as human sweat. The man was nearby.

Pausing, Tempe strained to hear something. Anything.

It struck her what a dangerous spot she was in. First, she had no idea who this man was or what he wanted. She didn't even know if he was the same person who had been following her and Abby. Hopefully, she had contacted the sheriff's department, but they weren't particularly enthusiastic about Abby or her. Maybe they wouldn't even respond. Though Tempe didn't always agree with her Sergeant or the detectives, they would definitely back her up in a situation like this.

Even if she did catch this guy, what could she do? Since he'd run from her, he clearly didn't want to talk to her. What on earth was she doing? The gun wasn't any use unless he actually threatened her life and that didn't seem to be his purpose. For that matter, what was his purpose?

A huge redwood log lay across the path. The only way to continue was to climb over it. Had the man she pursued done that, or was he lurking somewhere nearby?

Sniffing the air again, she caught the same scent of human sweat accompanied by leather and it seemed even closer.

Gathering her courage and with her hand on her revolver, Tempe said loudly, "Why don't you come out and tell me what you want?"

# CHAPTER 16

A man exploded from behind the huge trunk of a nearby redwood, nearly knocking her down as he pushed past her. She caught only a glimpse of his balding head and the leather jacket as he galloped back they way they'd come.

"Hey, wait," Tempe cried. "Talk to me. What is it you want to know?"

The man didn't slow down.

There was nothing for her to do but gallop after him though she knew she probably couldn't catch him. Hopefully, a deputy would be waiting somewhere near Abby's home and detain the man when he popped out of the woods.

It wasn't any easier retracing her steps then it had been getting there in the first place. If anything, the fog had descended lower to the ground. Feeling frustrated, and just a bit foolish, Tempe continued, wondering if she would ever make her way out of the forest.

When she'd decided she must have made a wrong turn and was hopelessly lost, the trees began to thin. Thank God. Despite the thick mist, she could see the asphalt of the street through the narrower trunks of the deciduous trees ahead.

Picking up her pace, Tempe darted out into the street, hoping to see a sheriff's car and the man she'd been chasing detained by a deputy.

A sheriff's car was parked in front of Abby's house, the deputy nowhere to be seen. In fact, as far as Tempe could see, the road was empty. Maybe, the man she'd been after was inside the house. Somehow, she doubted that would be the case.

Before she reached Abby's, she heard the sound of an engine roaring to life, and tires skidding on the gravel along the shoulder.

She stepped on Abby's porch as the door opened and a deputy Tempe had never seen before filled the doorway. Muscles strained his khaki uniform. Hatless, his sandy hair was cut short, his face handsome and unlined. He looked like a brand new high school graduate.

"Deputy Crabtree?" he asked. "I was about to go looking for you. Are you okay?"

Behind him, Abby stretched out her hands and looked toward the ceiling.

"Yes, I'm fine, but the man I was chasing got away. I wish you'd been outside. You might have been able to stop him. I just heard his car drive off."

The deputy, R. Johnson according to his name tag, frowned. "My instructions were to investigate a disturbance at Ms. Jacoby's home, and that's what I've been doing."

"Didn't anyone tell you that Ms. Jacoby and I have been followed and the man who has been following us turned up here tonight?"

The young man looked confused. "Well, yes, that's what she told me. But my sergeant said that we caught the guy who'd been following you. I was told to search for a prowler."

"The information you were given is incorrect. We're the ones who caught that fellow. The man Ms. Jacoby called about is someone new." Tempe spoke slowly, enunciating each word carefully.

Abby stepped closer. "I tried to tell him, but he was intent on walking around the house and searching inside."

Exasperated, Tempe said, "Did you hear anything I've been telling you? Listen carefully. I've been chasing a guy through the woods. He doubled back on me and got away. I heard him taking off in his car."

Deputy Johnson's cheeks turned bright red. He pulled a small notebook and pen out of his breast pocket. "Do you know what the car looked like?"

"It's a black Chevy sedan, fairly new," Tempe said.

The deputy made notes before he asked, "What or who is this guy after?"

Tempe shook her head. "That's the problem, I don't know. I think it's safe to assume he was interested in my involvement with Ms. Jacoby here and her friend, Ms. Mahoney."

He tipped his head and put his pen and notebook back in his pocket. "Indian stuff. That's out of our jurisdiction." He started for the door.

Tempe put her hands on her hips and blocked him. "What do you mean, out of your jurisdiction? Except for having dinner at one of the casinos, we haven't stepped foot on reservation or rancheria land since he's been on our tail."

"My sergeant gave me implicit instructions that I was not to get involved in any Tolowa business." The deputy tried to go around Tempe, but she moved directly in front of him again.

"Whatever is going on has nothing to do with the Tolowa. The only thing the three of us women have in common is that we are Native Americans. I never even heard of the Tolowa people until a few days ago. I think it's safe to say that whatever he wants doesn't have anything to do with them." Tempe's anger rose. "Are you telling me that if an Indian has a problem anywhere, the sheriff's department won't investigate?"

Deputy Johnson's face turned red. "I'm here, aren't I?"

"Lot of good you were. You let the man who has been harassing us get away, even though Ms. Jacoby explained to you what was going on."

"I was just following orders." The deputy side-stepped around Tempe.

Tempe wasn't going to let him go that easily. "How long have you been a deputy?"

His mumbled answer was almost unintelligible. "Six months."

"A rookie," Tempe exclaimed. "I've been a deputy for a lot longer. Let me give you some advice. After this, use your brain when you're investigating a call. Pay attention to what the reporting person has to say. You might actually save some-one someday."

By this time the deputy had reached his car. His last words were, "I was just following orders."

With hands on her hips, Abby said, "I could have told you that the sheriff's department wouldn't be helpful. I'm not surprised they sent a rookie. What does surprise me is that they sent anyone at all. If I hadn't mentioned you, they prob-ably wouldn't have. Too many of the deputies see Indians ei-ther as a nuisance, or in my case, the enemy. Not the majority of course, but you saw that there's bad blood between me and Sergeant Glade. Come in, I'm sure we'll be undisturbed the rest of the night."

Tempe agreed. Whoever she'd been chasing was long gone. Just the fact that the deputy's car was parked in front of the house, probably scared the man away—for the night at least. She stepped inside and Abby shut and locked the door.

"I only wish that I knew what this guy's motive is. I'm sure it has something to do with Vanessa's murder, but what, I haven't a clue."

Abby glanced at her watch. "If you're going to catch the early plane in the morning, you better get some sleep. Maybe, by the light of day, things will be clearer to you."

"I sure hope so. Except for getting to know you and Justine, I feel like I've been wasting my time up here. I sure haven't learned anything that is helpful to finding out who killed Vanessa."

"Don't try so hard, Tempe," Abby said. "I have a feeling when the time comes, you'll see your way clearly."

Tempe doubted that. As far as she knew, the solution to Vanessa Ainsworth's murder was as hard to discover as mak-ing her way through the redwood forest in the fog.

# CHAPTER 17

Tempe woke to the tantalizing scent of bacon, eggs and fresh coffee cooking. Before leaving, she called home to tell Hutch she would arrive later that day, and Sergeant Guthrie to let him know when the plane was due to land in Fresno, so someone would pick her up. Abby sent her off to the airport with a full stomach and a warm hug.

She arrived at the airport as the other passengers were hurrying out onto the tarmac. Displaying her identification and papers given to her by Sergeant Guthrie sped things along. She was the last one to climb the steps into the plane and her seat was near the front.

Upon arrival in San Francisco, Tempe grabbed her carry-on and followed behind the other passengers disembarking. Up ahead she spotted a familiar looking person wearing a leather jacket and baseball cap. The man she'd chased in the redwood forest. Could it possibly be him?

Tempe squeezed past a harried young mother with two small children. "Excuse me, please."

Stepping up her pace, Tempe took after the man. In the crowded concourse, she nearly caught up with him. "Sir, please, may I have a word with you?"

The man turned. Though he resembled the man Tempe had chased, this fellow didn't have a mustache.

Tempe paused and frowned. "Oh, I'm sorry, I thought you were someone else."

He mumbled and hurried away.

She stared after him. The more she watched, the more certain she was that he was the man who had followed her and Abby, the one she'd chased in the redwood forest. No doubt a phony mustache had been part of his disguise.

Glancing at her watch, she realized she only had a few minutes to get to her plane for Fresno which was leaving from a terminal in the opposite direction. Obviously this man wasn't going to talk to her, so there was no point in following him. She sighed and turned on her heel.

Striding down the moving walkway, Tempe followed the directions on the overhead signs to where she would catch her plane to Fresno. By the time she reached the correct spot, again the last of the other passengers disappeared through the door leading to the plane.

Sighing, she waved her boarding pass at the attendant who was starting to close the door. "I'm coming," she called.

Just before she reached the door, she turned her head. In the next waiting area, she spotted the now very familiar man with the baseball cap and black leather coat. It was too late to do anything about it.

∽≈

When she disembarked from the plane, she hurried toward the area outside of security where people waited for passengers. She expected to see a deputy from Tulare county; instead her heart leaped when she spotted Hutch's dark red hair, mussed as usual.

Grinning, she quickened her step. "Hutch. I didn't expect you."

He held out his arms to her. "I wanted to surprise you."

Embracing him, she said, "You certainly did that."

"How was your trip?"

"Interesting, but not productive."

He took her carry-on. "What do you mean? You didn't find out who murdered Vanessa?"

Tempe laughed. He must have thought she'd return with all the answers to the puzzle. "No, and I didn't really learn much to help solve Vanessa's murder. I'm afraid the detectives aren't going to be very happy."

While they waited for her other suitcase to arrive on the carousel, Hutch said, "The only way Sergeant Guthrie would let me come to get you was by making me promise to bring you straight to the department in Dennison. The detectives will be waiting to talk to you."

"It isn't going to take long, because I haven't got much to tell that will be helpful. What's been going on in Bear Creek?"

"Things are back to normal now that they have the fire mostly out. They have a few hot spots left, but everyone has returned home and I've pretty much got the church looking like it did before the emergency."

He brought her up-to-date on conditions people had found when they returned home. "The only structure that burned to the ground was at Vanessa's. The consensus is that the fire at her place was helped along by whoever killed her. No official word has been reported in the paper."

Suitcase retrieved, they made their way through the parking lot to Hutch's new white Chevy truck. "I still get a shock when I see your truck. I always expect to see your old red one."

"You and everyone else. I don't think anyone in Bear Creek believed I'd ever give up my faithful old truck." He put her suitcases in the backseat of the cab. "It wasn't easy, but it just got too expensive to keep running."

"I love your new truck," Tempe said. "And I love you much, much more." She kissed him before sliding into the seat.

When they left the airport and headed toward the freeway, Tempe said, "You've got to admit it's a lot more comfortable riding in this than your old truck."

Hutch laughed. "It's a lot faster too." He reached over and caressed Tempe's thigh.

"I'm so glad you're home."

"Me too, though I did have an interesting time. The woman I stayed with, Vanessa's cousin, Abigail, and her friend

Justine, treated me like they'd known me forever. Both women are fighting to make life better for the Tolowa and to help them remember their history."

Hutch glanced at Tempe. "Sounds interesting."

She told him what she'd learned about the tribe and how they'd nearly been exterminated. "It's hard to imagine."

"Nick Two John told me similar things happened to the Yokuts," Hutch said.

She was surprised. She hadn't heard anything about this before. "I wonder why he never told me."

Hutch shrugged. "He said that the Spaniards killed Indians indiscriminately as did the gold miners around Mariposa. Right in our own back yard, there was a battle in the mountains with the Yanduchi and the American soldiers from Fort Tejon."

"Oh, yes, I do remember hearing something about that when I was in high school."

"Genocide was definitely perpetrated against the Indians."

"Nick is right. I'm woefully ignorant about the history of my people."

"I'm sure you aren't the only one. What else did you do while you were there?"

"I had a meal in one of their casinos. And you'll be interested to know that Justine isn't fond of casinos either, though she knows some Indians gamble away their money, that's not her main reason for not liking them."

"Really? What else bothers her about them?"

"I'm not really sure. Basically, though, I think what bothers Justine and Abby most is that the Indians who work for the casino have turned their backs on their heritage. Instead they are focusing on material things that their salaries can buy."

"I'd like to meet this Justine. She sounds like an interesting woman."

"I invited her and Abby to come visit us some time. I think you'd like them both, although Justine isn't too fond of Christians."

"Maybe I could change her mind."

Tempe doubted that and changed the subject. "Did Blair call while I was gone?"

"No, but he seldom does during the week unless something unusual happens," Hutch reminded her.

"I just wondered."

The conversation changed again to things that were happening in Bear Creek. A new coffee shop was opening near the post office, and the woman who owned the gift store was planning to move back east to take care of her mother. Her store was up for sale. Hutch had been asked to perform a wedding for a young couple who attended his church and he'd set up marriage counseling sessions for the next four Saturdays. Now that the fire danger was nearly over, things were getting back to normal. Only a handful of out-of-town firemen remained to put out the hot spots.

Before long, Hutch pulled into the parking lot of the Dennison sheriff's sub-station.

"I'll wait out here. I'll do some studying." He popped open the glove compartment and brought out his Bible.

Tempe leaned over and kissed him on the cheek. "I don't think I'll be too long, I haven't much to tell them."

⤟❧

Detectives Morrison and Richards were waiting along with Sergeant Guthrie in the sergeant's office. They looked at up expectantly as she stepped inside.

Morrison's greeting was, "What did you find out?"

"Do you know who killed Ms. Ainsworth?" Richards asked.

"Take a seat, Crabtree," Sergeant Guthrie said. "How was your trip?"

Tempe knew he really didn't care. She opened her purse and pulled out the envelope with the money that was left in it, and put it on his desk. "Here's your money. I didn't spend much because I stayed at the home of Vanessa's cousin, Abigail Jacoby."

"We had a call from the Del Norte County sheriff's department, a Sergeant Glade. He didn't seem too thrilled about your presence in his territory," Guthrie said. "Sounded like you got under his skin."

"I don't think it was me that bothered him. He doesn't much like Abby or her friend, Justine. They are Indian rights activists, and Glade thinks they're troublemakers. Whether they are or not, I couldn't say. They were both very hospitable to me. Vanessa lived with Abby's family while she was growing up and Justine was her best friend."

"Then you must have discovered what we need to know to solve this case," Morrison said.

"Unfortunately, no. I found out a lot about Vanessa's earlier life, but nothing that will be helpful to you."

"Just tell us and we'll decide what's helpful or not." Richards squinted at her.

She described Vanessa's two boyfriends and how neither of them could be her murderer. "For awhile we were followed by a fellow named Lanny Hargrove who stalked Vanessa while she was in college."

"Sounds like our man," Richards said.

"Nope. He didn't even know Vanessa was dead. He was following us to find out where she was living now. When I told him what happened to her, he broke down and cried."

"Maybe he's a good actor," Morrison said.

Tempe ignored his remark. "After that someone else started following us."

"Oh yeah? Who was that?" Richards asked.

"I could never find out." She described her brief encounters with the man as well as his physical description. "I'm not even sure who he was following though it was probably me. I think he flew back on the same plane with me from Crescent City, though I didn't spot him until I reached San Francisco."

Richards started writing on a legal pad. "If he did fly back on the same plane with you, we ought to be able to find out who he was."

"I wonder how this guy knew you were in Crescent City,"

Morrison said.

"I don't think he did know. I think he might have been there for another reason and just happened to spot me with Abby. My thought was that he wanted to know what we were doing together."

"It has to have something to do with the murder," Richards said.

"Maybe so, but I sure can't figure it out. The two times I actually came face-to-face with the man, he didn't want to talk to me," Tempe said.

"What else did you find out?" Morrison asked.

"Besides what I learned about the Tolowa people, there really isn't anything."

"You must have missed something," Richards said.

"Or those women weren't telling you everything," Morrison said.

"No, they were very candid with me. Though they told me a lot about Vanessa's past life, there was nothing that will help solve her murder. What I did learn was that the only person who could possibly have a motive was her ex-husband."

Morrison shook his head. "His alibi is air tight. I guess we have to lean on her last boyfriend more."

"I don't think he did it." Tempe didn't know how to say it any plainer.

"Well, you sure didn't come up with anyone else," Richards said.

"No, I didn't. I've got a hunch if we could find out who was following me around we might learn what connection he has to the case."

"No doubt." Morrison crossed his arms over his massive chest and glared at Tempe. "Too bad you couldn't catch him."

"Believe me, I tried." She stood. "Can I go now? Hutch is waiting for me in the parking lot."

"Write a detailed report about what you learned," Sergeant Guthrie said. "You can send it via email. Maybe something will jump out at us. You can have the rest of the day off, but start your regular shift tomorrow."

Before she was completely out of earshot, Tempe heard Richards say, "We should have gone ourselves. Crabtree just didn't know what to look for."

*If that's what they wanted to think, fine.*

# CHAPTER 18

Hutch cooked dinner for Tempe. He served it by candlelight on the coffee table in the living room. Maybe things between them were improving, after all. They sat by each other on the couch covered with mismatched pillows. The rest of the furnishings were a combination of what she'd had before her marriage and what Hutch brought with him from his former house.

"It's great to have you home," he said, when they'd finished eating.

"I'm glad to be here."

"I know for awhile we haven't been as close as usual and I've been praying about that. I love you with all my heart."

"I love you too, Hutch. All of our disagreements about the casino drove us apart."

"I agree. The casino is here and nothing is going to change that. We shouldn't let it affect our marriage. I promise not to mention it anymore."

"It's there, so I don't know if you can actually never mention it again. I'd just be happy not to argue about whether it's good or bad."

Hutch gathered her in his arms and kissed her. "No more arguments about things that we have no influence over."

"Great."

"Something else has been missing too."

"I know." Tempe smiled at him. "I think we can fix that though, don't you agree?"

Hutch stood, took her by the hand and led her toward the bedroom.

"Shouldn't we clean up the dishes?" Tempe asked.

"Why? They'll be waiting for us in the morning."

Tempe was amazed. Hutch always wanted the dishes washed right after they ate. Perhaps things really were going to be different—maybe more like they had been when they were first married.

*≈*

Tempe would have liked to continue the romantic mood that had consumed her first night home, but it wasn't to be. Before she and Hutch finished with breakfast, he was called to the hospital to pray with a dying member of their church. Tempe did the dishes before sitting down at her computer to tackle her report about the trip to Crescent City.

Dutifully, she wrote down everywhere she went, who she met and their connection to Vanessa Ainsworth. Though she mentioned learning about the history of the Tolowa, she left out the details because they had nothing to do with Vanessa's murder. She wrote a complete run-down on both men who tailed her and Abby, noting that it became obvious Lanny had nothing to do with the murder. What the motive behind the second man's interest in her and Abby, Tempe couldn't figure out. Perhaps the detectives would learn his identity and from there come up with the answers. She'd done her part for the investigation into Vanessa's murder. Now it was back to her normal routine.

By the time she'd finished her report, and sent it as an e-mail to Sergeant Guthrie and the detectives, it was time to get ready for her shift. She'd received a call from Hutch that he'd have to stay at the hospital for awhile because the patient was critical and her relatives needed his support.

On duty, she cruised through Bear Creek, headed up the hill to the higher country, then came back down without a single call. Nothing suspicious seemed to be going on any-where, and she didn't even see anyone speeding. For a Saturday night, it was mighty dull, just as she liked it.

The Inn's parking lot had filled since she'd passed through town the first time. That was a good sign. Business was getting back to normal after the fire. She drove down the hill and decided to check out the new sports bar near the lake. A brightly-lit sign announced *Feldman's, Two Large Screen TVs*. Several trucks and SUVs, a couple of motorcycles and one bright yellow Hummer filled the parking lot.

She parked her Blazer and climbed out. Televisions dominated the medium-sized room, with one at each end of the bar. A young woman with fluffy blonde hair, wearing cut-off jean shorts exposing pudgy thighs, waited tables. Her light blue T-shirt was emblazoned on the back with Feldman's Sports Bar and Grill in large black letters. Eric Figueroa tended bar. When Tempe stepped inside, he made eye-contact with her.

"Hey, Deputy. What do you think?" he asked. He was clean-shaven and wore a T-shirt similar to the waitress's.

"About what?" Tempe asked. She nodded at several people she knew, cowboys in dirty Wranglers and Levis with their shirts sleeves rolled up, construction workers, also in soiled work clothes, all probably making the bar a detour on their way home.

Eric waved his hands. "This place. This is your first time here, isn't it?"

She glanced around. Though decorations were at a minimum, the tables and chairs were new. Everything looked clean. The smell of cooking beef and onions permeated the air. Customers consumed hamburgers and fries, some were drinking beer and others soda. "Nice. Looks like you're doing okay."

"We're keeping busy. Can I get you anything?" Eric asked.

"Those hamburgers sure look good." Tempe realized it was getting close to her dinner break. Wondering if Hutch was home yet, she said, "Get me two of those burgers to go." She slid onto a bar stool next to a young woman with long, dark hair who gave Tempe a dirty look. No doubt she'd been flirting with the handsome bartender and resented the intrusion.

Eric stepped into the kitchen for a moment to relay her order.

When he returned, Tempe said, "I just got back from Crescent City."

"Yeah?" Eric filled a glass with beer and put it on the waitress's tray.

"That's where Vanessa grew up."

"She never mentioned that to me," Eric said. "Why did you go up there? Do they know who killed her?"

"If by 'they', you mean the detectives, no, they don't. They sent me up there to see if I could find out anything that might help with the investigation."

"Did you?"

A big man in worn coveralls, a red bandana tied around his forehead, hollered, "Hey, Figueroa, how about a refill over here?"

Eric tended to his customer, then returned to stand in front of Tempe.

"Not really. What do you know about Vanessa's ex-husband?"

"I never met the guy, but Vanessa sure didn't like him. When we were together, he called her at least once a week to rag on her about the alimony payments. He didn't want to keep paying them, I guess. It was quite a bit of money, though I never knew how much."

"Did you tell the detectives this?"

"Sure, but they seemed far more interested in me and my activities. I certainly didn't have a motive to kill Vanessa, but my alibi stinks."

The waitress returned to the bar with more orders for beer and sodas. She fluffed her hair and batted her eyelashes at Eric. He filled the order, ignoring her flirtatious efforts.

When he turned back to her, Tempe said, "The husband has a great motive. The problem is he has an airtight alibi."

"Yeah, I know. And I don't."

⁂

Tempe was pleased to find Hutch's truck parked in the driveway. She'd always called their home a cottage because of its size and looks. Perched on top of a hill, built of dark weathered cedar planks, it was surrounded by ancient oaks, aspens, and cedars. Behind and below the house, Bear Creek rushed over a jumble of boulders and fallen logs.

She grabbed the bag with the hamburgers and French fries and went inside. In their small kitchen, with its rough-hewn cupboards and dark paneled walls, Hutch sat at the round table with a cup of coffee.

"I hope you haven't eaten yet," Tempe said. "I brought some hamburgers from the new sports bar."

"I wasn't hungry earlier. Mrs. Goss passed away. Even though they expected it, the family is pretty broken-up. It was very sad for them. We all know it's a blessing for her and she's now with the Lord, but they weren't ready for her to leave them."

Tempe kissed the top of Hutch's head. "Try one of these burgers. They smell wonderful. Eating one should make you feel better."

"You had a phone call," Hutch said.

"Blair?"

"No, it was Dr. Crandall, a woman."

"Oh, she's the crime scene investigator. I wonder what she wanted."

"Go ahead and call her back. Her phone number is there on the pad. I'll fix us something to drink. Do you want coffee? I made a fresh pot."

Tempe dialed the number. The phone only rang once before it was answered.

"Dr. Crandall here."

"This is Deputy Tempe Crabtree. You called me?"

"Oh, yes, Tempe. I wondered if the detectives shared my report with you."

Tempe laughed. "Of course not."

"I figured. Thought you'd like to know that both the dog and the victim were shot with the same gun. I did find the bullets so if anyone finds the gun at least we'll have something to work on. Unfortunately, the fire got rid of any clues that we might have had. Whoever shot Ms. Ainsworth and her dog did it a while before the fire reached her property. We found evidence that gasoline had been used as an accelerant around the studio and outside of the house. When the fire reached the area, despite the water drops, the foliage around the studio went up like tinder and enveloped the building."

"I felt sure Vanessa was killed before the fire reached her house because once it became obvious the fire threatened the buildings, the roads were closed to everyone but the fire-fighters," Tempe said.

"I'm sorry we don't know any more than we do. I hear that the department sent you to Crescent City to talk to her cousin. Did you find out anything interesting?"

"I learned plenty of fascinating information about Vanessa's childhood, a bit about her marriage and the Tolowa people, but nothing that would lead to the murderer. I suppose the oddest thing that happened is that I was tailed by two different men while I was there," Tempe said.

"What was that all about?" Dr. Crandall asked.

"The first guy was a fellow who had been in love with Vanessa since high school. He stalked her when she was in college and until she married."

"What about him as a suspect?"

"He is pretty weird, but he didn't even know she was dead. When he found out, he broke down completely. The reason he was following me was to see if he could find out where Vanessa is living now."

"You said there was a second person?"

"That guy was persistent. I actually caught up with him twice, but he fled before I could question him. I have no idea what that was all about. I think he might have been on the plane with me from Crescent City to San Francisco. Unfortunately, by the time I realized who he was it was too late to find out where he was going."

Dr. Crandall said nothing for a moment. "That's a bit scary.

That man might be Ms. Ainsworth's killer. I wonder why he was following you."

"I don't know and I'm not even sure it was me he was interested in because I was always with Vanessa's cousin, Abby Jacoby. He might have been interested in her rather than me and it was just a coincidence that he was in the airport."

"My feeling is it was you. You might be in some danger."

# CHAPTER 19

Tempe could think of no reason why anyone connected to Vanessa Ainsworth's murder would follow her. She knew absolutely nothing except what she'd learned in Crescent City—which didn't amount to much. In fact, nothing that would help identify Vanessa's killer.

Though she did have a strong feeling that despite his alibi, Vanessa's husband was responsible for her death. However, her part in the investigation was over. Now, whatever happened was up to the detectives.

Tempe summarized the phone call for Hutch, leaving out the doctor's warning. She glanced at her watch. "I'd better hurry and eat. I need to get back on duty."

The hamburger was the best she'd ever had, and Hutch agreed. She'd make it a point to tell Eric the next time she saw him.

The rest of Tempe's shift consisted of a domestic violence call that turned out to be non-physical, merely an argument that became loud enough to bother the neighbors. The result was that the feuding couple immediately made-up and expressed their anger toward their meddling neighbors. Tempe warned, "I don't want to be called back here because you're fighting again, or that you've become a problem to your neighbors."

She handed out two speeding tickets, both to men she knew who hadn't bothered to slow down when they entered the town part of Bear Creek. It always amazed her how polite most men were when she gave them a ticket. Both of these fellows told her thank-you when she handed the citation to them. She couldn't keep from smiling when she said, "You're welcome."

Kids playing in the park after ten caught her attention. She knew all three of the tow-headed and blue-eyed children from the trailer park. The girl was ten, her brothers six and seven. "What are you doing here so late?"

"We weren't doing nothing wrong," the girl said, standing tall. Her brothers tried to hide behind her, their eyes huge.

"It's not safe for you to away from home when it's dark," Tempe said. "Come hop into my Blazer and I'll take you home."

"Uh-uh," the little girl said. "My mom'll be mad if we do."

"Where is your mother?" Tempe asked.

"Sleeping."

Tempe remembered that their mom was single and worked at the school as an aide and also cleaned houses in order to feed her family and pay the rent. "What were you supposed to be doing?" Tempe asked.

"Watching my brothers and keeping them quiet. That's why we came to the park to play so we wouldn't wake her up."

"Tell you what. I'll take you home, but I won't talk to your mom. Just go in the house and get into bed. But I never want to catch you outside after dark again, okay?" She wouldn't talk to her mom tonight, but she'd make a point to let her know what her children had done. She also wanted to make sure that there wasn't any other reason that the children had left the house so late.

Her next call was a car burglary. The victim was the owner of a Cadillac Escalade parked in the circular driveway of a new, extremely large home. Though Tempe had seen the man around town, she'd not met him.

He waited beside the black Escalade as she drove in. Upon Tempe's exit from her Blazer, he ran to her. "I can't believe it. They took all my CDs, the money I had in my glove compartment and all my tools out of the back."

"Was the vehicle locked?" Tempe asked.

The man's face turned red. "No. I never lock my car when it's in front of my house."

"You'll start doing it after this, I suspect."

She told him to go into the sub-station in the morning and bring all the information about the stolen items with him. It was always the same with people who had moved to Bear Creek from Southern California. For some reason, they seemed to think they'd left crime behind. It didn't help when they made it too simple for someone easily tempted.

As she drove from the mountainous areas, down by the lake and back again, she couldn't help but think about Vanessa's murder. She wondered just what Acton Ainsworth's airtight alibi was and if there was any way she could find out.

When she arrived home, Hutch was in bed and asleep. The reading light on the night stand was still on. His glasses lay atop his Bible. She studied him for a moment. The sight of his rumpled auburn hair, the freckles scattered over his lightly tanned cheeks, and the slight smile on his lips tugged at her heart. She loved him so much. It seemed as though their relationship was definitely on the mend. She leaned over and kissed him lightly on the forehead. His smile broadened, but he didn't wake up.

Though tired, Tempe decided to do a search for Acton Ainsworth's name on the Internet. As she'd expected, the first things that came up were references to his many stores located from San Diego to Ukiah. She even found a photo showing him standing in front of his Santa Barbara store. He was tall, handsome, with a full head of sandy hair. An enormous grin displayed lots of white teeth. He looked like the successful business man that he was, not a wife-murderer.

She scanned more and found stories about an annual golf-tournament Ainsworth headed where the proceeds went to an organization for autistic children. There were more photographs with Ainsworth displaying his toothy grin.

Almost ready to stop, Tempe spotted a heading, "Local

Philanthropist Runs Afoul of the Law." The article was attrib-
uted to the Santa Barbara Daily News. But when she clicked
on it, the words *No Longer Available* popped up.

Darn. She wondered how she could find out what that
was all about. Probably the only way would be to go to Santa
Barbara. She'd never get permission from Sergeant Guthrie,
and certainly, Hutch wouldn't approve. Sighing, she exited the
search engine. It was time to join Hutch in bed.

She didn't know how long she'd been asleep, when she
heard, "Tempe." And again, "Tempe."

# CHAPTER 20

Opening her eyes, she peered around. The room was dark, only a splinter of pale light came through a gap where the window curtains didn't quite come together. A shadowy figure stood at the end of the bed.

Tempe sat up. Her heart beat quickened. She blinked, trying to focus, not believing what she was seeing. "Who are you?"

The short-cropped graying hair was feathery, the features not substantial. Only the eyes stood out. They seemed to be pleading.

"Vanessa?" How could it be? Vanessa was dead. "What do you want?"

Beside her, Hutch turned toward her, "What's going on? Who are you talking to?"

"I'm not sure. It looks like Vanessa." Tempe said.

Hutch raised up on one elbow and peered toward the figure. He frowned and rubbed his eyes.

Whatever it was faded, becoming nothing more than an outline, then vanished completely.

"Did you see her?" Tempe asked.

"I'm not sure what I saw," Hutch said.

"But you *did* see something, right?"

"A shadow. I don't know exactly. What did you see?"

"I think it was Vanessa."

Hutch made no comment.

Tempe knew he didn't believe in ghosts or speaking to spirits, or at least he didn't think people should try to conjure them for any reason.

"I was sleeping. She called my name, that's what woke me up," Tempe said.

"Did she say what she wanted?"

Tempe studied his face to see if he was being sarcastic. But his expression was open and curious. "No, but the way she looked at me, it was like she was pleading."

"To do what?" he asked.

"I have no idea."

Hutch glanced at the clock next to his Bible. "It's nearly four a.m."

"I'm sorry I woke you. I know you have to preach in the morning. Go back to sleep, sweetheart."

"Do you want to talk about it? It's okay, really," Hutch said.

Tempe sighed. "I don't think it will help. I don't know why she appeared to me."

"I'm sure her tragic death is heavy on your mind, especially after traveling to her hometown and learning so much about her," Hutch said. "Maybe your imagination conjured her."

"Maybe," Tempe said, though she knew in her heart that it was Vanessa's spirit or essence that had awakened her from a sound sleep. She scrunched under the covers and cuddled next to Hutch.

He kissed her and smoothed her hair. "I love you." His eyes closed and it wasn't long until his breathing was deep and even.

Tempe found it difficult to fall asleep. There was only one reason for Vanessa to make her appearance; obviously she wanted Tempe to find her killer. Though Tempe would like to do just that, the odds of her having the opportunity were none at all.

❧❧

Hutch was shaving when Tempe stepped into the bathroom and put her arms around him.

"How are you this morning?" he asked, as he pulled the razor up his cheek.

"Great. I'll get ready and go to church with you."

"Super." Hutch rinsed shaving cream from the razor. "Everyone will be happy to see you. We have much to be thankful for today with that horrible fire finally out."

"I wish that things had been different for Vanessa."

Hutch turned and took her in his arms. "I know you do."

When he released her, she had shaving cream on her nose and one cheek. She giggled.

"I'll take my shower now," Tempe said.

Before she could get in the shower, the phone rang. "Go ahead," Hutch said. "I'll get it."

She'd pulled off her nightshirt, but hadn't stepped into the shower yet when Hutch brought the phone to her. "It's for you."

The voice on the phone was young and hysterical. "Someone killed Pansy!"

"Try to calm down. Who is this?"

"Erin Lindquist."

Tempe knew the Lindquist family included several children from high school age down to a toddler. "Okay, Erin, tell me what happened. Who is Pansy?" She had a horrible vision of one of the children lying dead.

"Pansy's my pig. Someone stabbed her." The girl broke down, sobbing.

A male voice came on the phone. "This is Erin's father, John Lindquist. Pansy is the pig Erin is…was raising for 4 H. When Erin went down to feed her this morning, someone had gutted her. Blood is everywhere. Naturally Erin is very upset. Who would do such a thing?"

Tempe had no answer. "Tell me exactly where you live and I'll be there in a few minutes. Don't let anyone touch a thing."

"Don't worry. I don't want the other kids to see. I'd like to get my hands on the freak that would do such a horrible thing."

"I hope we can find out who did it. Tell me exactly where

you live. And, please, keep everyone in the house."

Hutch stood there expectantly. "Sounds like you won't be making it to church."

She explained what happened. "My shower will have to wait too."

Smiling, Hutch said, "I do hope you plan to get dressed first."

Tempe looked down at her naked body and nodded. "Oh, yes."

Hurriedly, Tempe put on her uniform and brushed her hair while Hutch finished dressing and headed for the kitchen. "Do you want me to fix you something to eat?"

"No, I don't have time. If this doesn't take too long, I might still be able to make it to church."

"I won't count on it."

Hutch stood at the stove in the kitchen scrambling eggs when Tempe came out. She looped her long braid and fastened it to the back of her head. Kissing Hutch on the cheek, she said, "Say a little prayer for Erin. I know she is really upset. I can't imagine why anyone would do such a horrible thing."

She opened the back door.

A dark red heart lay in a puddle of blood on the doorstep. She screamed, "Oh, my God."

Hutch came up behind her. "What is it?" He peered over her shoulder. "Is that what I think it is?"

"I'm afraid so." She leaned against him for a moment, a million questions bombarding her.

"But it's not a human heart, right?"

"I don't think so." No matter whether it was or not she'd have to call in and report it.

She shook her head. Though it looked like one, she felt sure it wasn't from a human. "I'm pretty sure I know where it came from."

"Erin's pig," Hutch said.

"Has to be. But why? Why kill a pig, cut out its heart and leave it at our door?"

"Is this something for the detectives to investigate?"

"I think they'd probably laugh at me if I called them about the death of a pig."

Hutch placed his hand on her shoulder. "But this is some kind of a threat to you, isn't it? Why else would someone put a bloody heart in front of your house?"

"Why indeed? I have no idea." She stared at the heart for a long moment. "I have a feeling I was supposed to find the heart before I heard about the pig. It does looks like a human heart, doesn't it?"

"I suppose, though I haven't seen any actual human hearts lately…or ever, really. Just in pictures."

"Speaking of pictures, I'll have to take photographs of this, treat it as much like a crime scene as I can. See if I can find any clues, though I doubt there will be any. Then I'll let Sergeant Guthrie know what's going on. Please go back inside and give the Lindquists a call. You'll have to look their number up in the phone book. Let them know I've been delayed."

Taking a wide birth around the bloody heart, Tempe went to her Blazer and got her camera. She took several pictures of the heart from different angles. Their cottage was on a corner with no close neighbors on either side. The house across the street was completely out of view because set back behind a wall of thick bushes and tall trees. No one around to ask if they'd seen anyone acting suspiciously.

Everything looked exactly as it always did. Her vehicle sat in the gravel driveway beside Hutch's new truck. Except for her ghostly visitor, Tempe hadn't been disturbed by any unusual activity in the night.

Going back into the house, Tempe asked, "Hutch, did you hear a car outside earlier this morning?"

"Except when you woke me at four, I didn't hear anything until the alarm woke me."

"Me either." Of course that wasn't unusual, living on a corner as they did, they were used to the sounds of vehicles passing by.

"What are you going to do now?" Hutch asked.

"Collect the evidence."

Hutch stared at her for a moment. "The heart?"

"Yes, I'll have to make sure that the heart actually came from the pig." She certainly prayed that it was the pig's heart. Otherwise she'd be tampering with evidence. She shook her head to rid herself any doubt. That was the only explanation for the bloody mess on her porch

Hutch found a small cardboard box for her. She lined it with newspapers. Putting on disposable gloves, she scooped the gruesome object into the box. As she carried the box to the Blazer, Hutch asked, "Will it be okay to hose off the blood now?"

"Sure." Tempe said.

"Good luck," Hutch called after her.

≈≈

The Lindquists' home was only a couple of miles away, up the winding road past several small ranches. The entrance to their home was marked by a signpost with the name *Lindquist* painted on it along with the house number, and dangling from it, a sign with the 4-H symbol. On either side of the lane were grassy fenced-in pastures. One held a cow and calf, and on the other, two grazing horses. As Tempe drove to the house, she passed several small outbuildings and fenced enclosures. No doubt one held the slaughtered pig.

She parked her car in front of a large white house with a covered porch. As she started up the wide steps, the front door popped open and children of all ages spilled out.

"Someone killed Erin's pig," a wide-eyed boy of about five exclaimed.

"Pansy won a prize at the fair," said an older girl, about twelve and wearing glasses.

Another boy, who looked the same age as the girl, shoved his way in front of the others. "But she wouldn't sell Pansy because she didn't want anyone to eat her."

One girl leaned against her father, Mr. Lindquist, his arm around her. Slightly younger than the girl with glasses, she had straight, silky blonde hair. The end of her pug nose was red and her eyes swollen. Obviously, Erin.

He extended his free hand to Tempe. "Carl Lindquist." He glanced down toward the daughter he comforted. "This is Erin."

"Hi, Erin. Tell me what happened this morning."

Between great shudders and sniffing, Erin began her story. "This morning…I went down to feed Pansy…like I always do. I knew something was wrong….right away. Soon as she heard me coming…she always came up to the fence…making her snorting noises." Erin put her head against her father's chest and wept.

"This is really hard on my daughter. She treated Pansy like a pet."

Erin wiped at her nose and eyes with the back of her hand. "She was more than a pet. I loved Pansy and Pansy loved me."

"I know this is hard for you, Erin, but I need to know what happened next."

"When I didn't hear her saying 'hello,' I knew something was wrong. I thought she might be sick. I hopped up on the fence to see and there she was." Erin broke down again.

Mr. Lindquist hugged his daughter for a moment. "Try to go on, honey. Deputy Crabtree needs to know what you saw if she's going to find out who did this."

Through the tears, Erin said, "Pansy was just laying there in the pen. She was cut open and all bloody down the front of her."

"Did you see anything else that was unusual?" Tempe asked.

"No. I just screamed and ran back to the house and called you." Her sobs came from deep within.

"Perhaps you ought to be the one to show me the pig, Mr. Lindquist," Tempe said. "But before we do, did any of the rest of you kids hear or see anything during the night or early this morning?"

The children all shook their heads except the older boy.

"Grizzly woke me up barking. I don't know what time it was, but it was still dark outside."

Mr. Lindquist said, "Grizzly's a border collie. We have to keep him inside. He chases every wild critter that noses around here. I'm afraid he might tangle with something too big for him to handle."

"Did you hear him barking last night?"

"He barks every night, Deputy. He sleeps in the boys' room. They seem to be able to sleep through the ruckus better than any of the rest of us. If I heard him, I didn't pay any attention."

"Let's go down and take a look at the pig," Tempe said.

All of the children started to follow, but Mr. Lindquist said, "All of you, go inside with your mother. Deputy Crabtree doesn't need you trampling any clues that might be there."

Tempe doubted she'd find any clues, but she was happy not to have the kids going with them. That they were disappointed was evidenced by their protests.

Mr. Lindquist frowned at them sternly and they disappeared into the house. "It's this way." He led Tempe back through a gate in the fence, past a neat vegetable garden and down a sloping hill towards the out-buildings she'd spotted on her way to the house. The first small building was surrounded by a wire fence that corralled several chickens and one rooster.

As they approached the second building, a bit larger than the first, Tempe could smell the blood. This area had a wooden fence with horizontal slats and a large gate. Mr. Lindquist swung the gate open.

The first thing Tempe saw was the huge pig, feet in the air, a gaping slit down it's belly, flies already buzzing around the bloody mess. "Has anyone been in there besides Erin?"

"I don't think she actually stepped inside this morning. She peeked over the fence and saw Pansy and came screaming to the house."

"How often does she clean down here?" The area was filled with straw, not much of it dirtied. Though some of it looked like it had been mashed down, there weren't any obvious shoe prints.

"Erin loves...loved Pansy. She was down here a lot. She cleaned out the dirty hay and put down fresh every day. She kept Pansy clean. If the pig hadn't gotten so big, she'd have been begging to bring her in the house. When Pansy was a piglet, she stayed in Erin's room at night until she got too heavy for Erin to carry around."

Mr. Lindquist hung his head and jammed his hands in his pocket. "We should have insisted that Erin sell that pig at the fair. Then she wouldn't be going through this now. Who do you think could have done such a horrible thing?"

"I have no idea. Take a good look at Pansy. What do you see?"

Frowning, Mr. Lindquist stared at Tempe. "What do you mean? She's been slaughtered."

"Yes, I know, but look at how she's been cut open. What does it look like to you?"

He stared at the mutilated pig. "It just looks like someone who didn't know what they were doing hacked that pig with something sharp."

"Yes. But do you see anything missing?" Tempe asked.

"I don't know what you mean. If someone was going to kill the pig for food, he'd have taken a hunk of her, something that could be cooked."

"Come back with me to my Blazer. I want to show you something."

Looking puzzled, Mr. Lindquist followed Tempe.

She opened the passenger door and opened the box she'd put on the seat. "Take a look at this and see if you think it belonged to Pansy."

As she held open the box, he peered inside. "Oh my Lord, that's got to be Pansy's heart. Where did you find it?"

"When I came outside this morning planning on coming to your house, it was on my front step."

Slowly, he shook his head. "I don't understand."

"Neither do I. I'm guessing this is supposed to be some

kind of message to me, but what, I haven't a clue. I'm sure it has nothing to do with your family. Unfortunately, the pig was handy. Whoever the sicko is has something against me."

"Oh, my goodness. I don't know what to say."

"I'm not sure I do either. How about keeping your family inside for awhile? How much you want to tell them is up to you. I'd like to look around that pig's pen a bit and see if I can find anything. I really don't expect to."

"Of course, Deputy. One thing I'd like to ask you though. When can I bury the pig? It's going to be stinking pretty soon, and I know that Erin will want to give Pansy a proper funeral."

# CHAPTER 21

Tempe decided to call Sergeant Guthrie at home and find out what he thought about the whole situation. "May I use your telephone? I need to call my sergeant."

"Of course. You can use the phone in my study." Mr. Lindquist escorted her inside the spacious living room. That the house was occupied by several children was obvious by the toys, books and clothing scattered around on the mismatched tables and worn but comfortable looking couches and chairs.

All the Lindquists' blond children were gathered around a large picnic-style table. They'd obviously been eating before Tempe and their father entered, but now they stared at her with big, curious eyes. All except Erin, at the end of the table. Her head was bowed, hair falling over her face. Mrs. Lindquist, a pretty, young woman, stood between the table and the stove. "Children, eat your breakfast."

Her offspring ignored the request and continued to stare.

Mr. Lindquist satisfied part of their curiosity. "Deputy Crabtree needs to use the phone." He led her to the other end of the living room, opened a door, and motioned her inside. "The telephone is on the desk. I'll close the door and give you some privacy."

Though the room was small compared to the other two, it was large enough to hold a massive mahogany desk, a comfortable chair, and a small leather couch. Three walls were covered with bookcases holding leather-bound classics, some best sellers, and books on engineering, a clue to Mr. Lindquist's occupation, perhaps.

Tempe picked up the receiver and dialed Sgt. Guthrie's home number. She was grateful to hear the sergeant's voice when he answered. Mrs. Guthrie always expressed her annoyance when her husband was called at home.

"This is Tempe Crabtree. I have a situation up here that I need some advice about."

"What's that?" He didn't sound too happy to be disturbed.

"Sir, someone has slaughtered a pig and…"

"You called me about a pig?"

"Yes, sir, it was a girl's pet."

Before she could say anymore, Guthrie snapped, "Maybe someone was hungry for a ham dinner."

She spoke quickly so he wouldn't interrupt her again. "No sir. You see, whoever did it, only took the pig's heart. This morning when I went outside, I found it on my doorstep."

There was a long silence. "Oh. And you're sure the heart is from that pig?"

"Reasonably so, sir. What do you want me to do? The little girl who owned the pig is anxious to give it a burial."

"Did you find any evidence either around your house or where the pig was killed?"

"Nothing at my house, though I have taken photographs. I haven't done that here yet."

"Take pictures of that pig and its surroundings. Do a good search, see if you can find anything. Then go ahead and let the kid bury her pig."

"Thank you sir. I'll do that."

"One more thing, Crabtree, do you have any idea why someone would put that pig's heart on your doorstep?"

"No, sir, I don't."

"It'd be mighty helpful if you could find whatever the killer used to cut into the pig."

"Yes, sir, it would."

"Get busy. Write a full report and bring it and the pictures in tomorrow."

"Yes, sir." Another day off spoiled.

After thanking the Lindquists for the use of the phone, Tempe added, "I'll be outside taking some pictures and looking around for a bit. I'd appreciate it if the children stayed inside until I'm through."

Tempe returned to the scene of the crime with her digital camera around her neck, carrying the box with the heart in it, and disposable gloves. Standing outside the open gate, she took her time studying the tableau before her. Except for the butchered pig's carcass and the bloodied straw, nothing looked unusual or out of place. Putting the box on the ground, she took several photos from outside the fence. As she walked the perimeter, she looked for anything out of the ordinary.

The ground was hard and dry from lack of rain. The small enclosure for the pig was made of boards and had been painted white like the house. A brightly painted sign with purple flowers on the border and the name "Pansy" hung over the entrance.

Nothing caught Tempe's interest as she walked all the way around until she came back to where she'd begun at the gate.

Sighing, she slipped on the gloves. She stepped inside the pig's compound and walked all around, avoiding the surprisingly few pig droppings. Near Pansy's sty, under the shelter of the overhanging roof, was a nearly empty food trough and a half-full galvanized water bucket. Tempe peeked inside the shed and found more nearly clean hay—but nothing else.

Standing over the pig, Tempe photographed the gaping, bloody hole. Then she retrieved the box from outside the fence. Reaching in with her gloved hands, Tempe lifted out the heart. She carefully set it inside the gory cavity. It fit quite nicely.

She pulled off the gloves so they were inside out, rolled them up inside each other and dropped them in the now empty box. Lifting the camera, she took several more pictures of the reunited heart and its owner.

Not knowing anything else to do, she stepped out of the pen. Shading her eyes from the brightness of the morning sun, she looked toward the house and then back to the road. It would have been an easy task for someone to park on the road, hike up the lane, climb over the fence and slaughter the pig. The pig's pen was far enough away from the house that even if the pig had made a noise when she was killed, the family wouldn't have heard it.

Before Tempe left, she knocked on the door and asked the boy who answered, "May I please speak with your father?"

"Hey, dad, the lady wants to talk to you again." The boy scampered away, leaving the door open.

When Mr. Lindquist appeared, Tempe said, "You can go ahead and have your funeral. Be careful though, I put the pig's heart back where it belongs."

"Thank you. Did you find out anything?" he asked.

"Not really," Tempe said. "If you should run across anything that's out of place, please let me know."

"I'll do that, Deputy."

By the time she returned home, Hutch had left for church. She glanced at her watch. The service had already started. Instead of trying to go, she took a shower and wrote her report for Sergeant Guthrie.

By the time Hutch arrived home, she'd finished the report and was wondering what to fix to eat.

With a huge grin on his face, Hutch greeted her. "I'm so glad you're home. Why don't we pop up to the Inn for dinner?"

On Sunday, their big meal was always after church. Glancing at the dark blue mid-calf pants and blue T-shirt she'd put on after her shower, she said, "I guess I look respectable enough to be seen with you."

For the morning service at church, one Sunday Hutch wore a dress shirt and tie and the next he'd wear slacks and a nice shirt without a tie. He liked to please both the older members of his flock who always wore their Sunday best and those who dressed in a more relaxed fashion. This was the day for the more casual attire.

"You are gorgeous no matter what you're wearing." He

gave her a kiss and hug. "Let's get going, I'm starved."

As usual on Sunday, the Inn was crowded. Many of the people who attended the Bear Creek Community Church regularly were already seated. Claudia Donato, the owner of the Inn and Nick Two John's "significant other", greeted them warmly. As usual, the woman's abundant blond hair was coifed in the latest style, her make-up perfect. She wore a dark blue suit with a glittery silver and blue silk scarf that flowed behind her. She led them across the polished wood floor to a small table in the middle of the room. Nearly everyone spoke to them as they passed.

"I'm sorry you can't have a table near the window. I know that's what you prefer," Claudia said, as she handed them their menus. "We're just too crowded."

"I'm so hungry, I'd be willing to sit in the kitchen if you didn't have room." Hutch grinned.

Claudia smiled her perfect smile. "Don't worry, we'll always have a place for you and Tempe. Enjoy your meal."

When she was gone, Tempe asked, "How was church?"

"I thought it went well. We had a good crowd. People asked about you, of course."

"Since I only manage to get there about half the time, they probably don't think too kindly of me."

"I'm sure everyone understands about your job. Certainly enough of them have required your services at times. Tell me about the pig. Did you find out anything?"

"Nothing helpful. The poor girl that it belonged to is heartbroken. She loved that pig as much as any kid loves her pet. I felt so sorry for her."

"What's going to happen with it?"

"They're going to give it a proper pet funeral."

A girl in her early twenties appeared before them, dressed in a white blouse and black slacks. She pulled an order pad and pen from the pocket of a small apron. "May I take your drink orders?"

Hutch turned to Tempe. She ordered ice tea. "Me too," he said. "We better decide what we want to eat."

While they were studying the menu, the waitress brought back their drinks. "The specials today are Herb and Applesauce Glazed Pork Chops and Blackberry Salmon."

Tempe had to repress a grimace. "I'll have the salmon."

"Sounds good to me too."

After they'd made their choices for salad and dressing, Hutch choosing a baked potato and she the parsleyed red potatoes, the waitress left. Tempe leaned across the table, "I don't think I'll ever be able to eat a pork chop again."

❧❧

The phone was ringing when Tempe and Hutch returned home. Hutch answered and handed it to Tempe.

She mouthed, "Who is it?"

Hutch shrugged.

She took the phone. "This is Deputy Crabtree."

"Detective Morrison here. Just heard about the pig's heart. Sounds like someone doesn't like you. Did you give the wrong person a ticket?" He chuckled.

Tempe decided to ignore his comment and said nothing.

After a long pause, Morrison said, "I'd like to talk to you, privately. I've got an idea about this case."

"My shift starts at four," Tempe said.

"Not today. I was thinking I could meet you somewhere for coffee tomorrow."

"I'm supposed to have Monday off and I already have to take my report and pictures to Sergeant Guthrie."

"This won't take long and I think you'll want to hear what I have to say. I'll come up there. How about that little hamburger joint right on the highway. Bring the report and pictures to me and you won't have to make the trip to town. I'll see you at ten." He hung up before she could protest further.

"What now?" Hutch asked.

"That was Detective Morrison. He wants to meet me for coffee tomorrow."

"Why?"

"I have no idea." It certainly wasn't like Morrison to discuss a case with her. He never acted like he even liked her. And she couldn't think of a time she'd ever seen Morrison without Detective Richards.

She'd just have to wait until tomorrow to find out what the detective wanted.

# CHAPTER 22

Once again Tempe's sleep was disturbed. The wraith that resembled Vanessa Ainsworth called out to Tempe, waking her. This time Vanessa seemed to have more substance, though she certainly didn't resemble a living being, nor did she appear like the ethereal spirits displayed in movies and TV. Tempe had no doubt that the specter hovering before her was the essence of Vanessa.

Once Tempe was awake enough to react, she asked in a quiet voice, so as not to wake Hutch, "What is it you want from me, Vanessa?"

The ghostly expression was sad and a silvery tear slid down the pale cheek before she faded away.

In the morning, Tempe told Hutch Vanessa had made another appearance. "I wish I knew what she wanted."

His reaction was surprising. "Why don't you find Nick Two John and ask him?"

"Really? You think I should?"

"If anyone can help you with this, Nick can."

"After I talk to Detective Morrison, I'll go by the Inn."

❧❧

At The Café, Detective Morrison's bulk nearly filled one side of a booth. Tempe pushed open the door and approached. To emphasize the fact that this was supposed to be one of her days off, she wore her dark hair down, her black jeans, and an aqua turtleneck sweater.

When he spotted her, Morrison stood. Surprisingly, he grinned, softening his features and making him appear less formidable. He wore his usual, a tweed sport jacket over a checked shirt and wrinkled tan slacks. As she approached, he greeted her warmly. "Thanks for coming, Crabtree. I already ordered you a cup of coffee. Hope that's okay."

"Thanks." She handed him a manila envelope with her report and photos she'd printed from her computer. "Be sure Sergeant Guthrie gets these." She slid into the booth across from him as he sat down. "What's this all about, Detective?"

Instead of answering, he opened the envelope, pulled out the photographs she'd taken and glanced at each one before dropping them back inside. He set the envelope on the table away from his coffee cup. "Guthrie called me about the pig's heart. Bet that was a shock."

"Definitely." She waited expectantly.

"I hope you're taking it seriously."

"What do you mean?"

"It's a warning. You're in danger."

"I suppose you're right, but I sure don't know who is behind it."

"That's what I want to talk to you about."

"I gathered as much."

Morrison cradled his cup with his big hands. "I realize I haven't been particularly nice to you."

She decided not to respond to his comment and merely waited.

"We have a lot more in common than you think," he began.

Besides being in law enforcement, Tempe couldn't think of anything they could possibly share. "Really."

"I understand your first husband was a highway patrolman."

Tempe nodded.

"My father was a CHP. Like your husband he was killed in the line of duty. Made a traffic stop and was shot by the driver."

"Oh, I'm sorry," Tempe said. She realized she didn't know anything about Morrison except that he was a detective. She'd judged him as an uncaring and emotionless man based only on how he acted with her. But why was he telling her all this? Most of the time he couldn't bother to tell her hello or goodbye. Obviously he had something he wanted her to do and was trying to win her over by gaining her sympathy.

He continued. "It happened when I was sixteen years old. I had two younger brothers and a sister. My mother was devastated. She'd always been a stay-at-home mom. Though she received my dad's insurance it wasn't really enough for such a big family. Her goal was for all of us to go to college. Football was my game and I did well enough to get a scholarship to Fresno State. Once I got there, I took classes in law enforcement. Mom had a fit, of course. Couldn't understand why I'd want to do something that would put my life in danger. She even encouraged me to go into professional football, but I wasn't interested. I'd been battered around enough after four years of college ball. By the time I graduated from the police academy, she let me know how proud she was."

Despite her suspicions about his motive, Tempe began to see Morrison as a human being, not the adversary she'd always considered him. "I'm sure she's even more proud of you now."

He lowered his eyes. "She died of cancer last year."

"Oh, I'm sorry." Doubt nipped at Tempe. Why was Morrison telling her all this? Was he trying to soften her up for some reason? She sipped her coffee.

"That was tough, but she'd been really sick for awhile and we all knew it was coming. In any case, it's always hard to lose your mother."

"Yes, I know. My mom is gone too."

"I heard."

Tempe wondered about that. Who had given Morrison this information about her? Probably Sergeant Guthrie, but why would Morrison care?

"Guthrie and I discussed this pig heart business. Obviously, someone wants to put the fear of God in you."

"But why?" Tempe asked.

The waitress, an older woman, came by and topped off Tempe's and Morrison's coffee. Though usually extremely friendly and talkative, she must have realized the conversation was serious and didn't interrupt.

"If you haven't ticked off anyone around here, then it has to have something to do with the Ainsworth murder case. Since we have no real leads at this time, it makes this threat to you rather important."

"I don't see how. What good does it do if I don't know who is threatening me?"

Morrison lifted his cup to his lips and drank. "Whoever it is didn't like it that you went up to Crescent City to see Vanessa Ainsworth's cousin and friend. It has to be someone connected to the case. The only possibility is her husband, despite his alibi."

"I found a photograph of Acton Ainsworth on the Internet and I can assure that wasn't who was following me around."

"Ainsworth is well-off enough to hire someone to follow you and take care of anything else he wants done." Morrison's stared at her, his eyes dark beneath his protruding forehead.

Tempe stared back at him, and without thinking said, "Like hiring someone to kill his wife."

Grinning, Morrison said, "Exactly. I guessed you might see it the same way I do."

So what if she did. Why was he sharing with her? She felt it best to keep silent and let Morrison do the rest of the talking.

Deep wrinkles formed on his lumpy face.

Tempe guessed he was thinking about what to say next. He took so long, she started to slide out of the seat. "If that's all, I guess…"

Morrison grabbed her wrist with his big hand. "Wait. I haven't finished."

"Okay." She scooted back in place.

He released his grip on her. "I don't know if you'll want

to do this."

"Do what?"

"Go to Santa Barbara." His dark gaze fixed on her again.

"Why?"

"The only way we're going to get this guy is to draw him out."

"By this guy, do you mean the killer or Acton Ainsworth?" Tempe asked.

"Either one…or both."

"In other words, what you want me to do is become a target."

# CHAPTER 23

"I wouldn't exactly put it that way," Morrison said.

"I would." Tempe stared back at him with the same force-fulness he was using on her.

Morrison reached up and scratched a battered ear. Though he looked like the former football player he had been, Tempe wasn't sure that was how he'd earned his battered looks. He said, "I thought you'd jump at the chance to do this. You never seemed to have any trouble in the past going out on a limb to look for the bad guy."

"Maybe so, but I did it because it seemed to me you were going after the wrong person."

Again, his surprisingly engaging grin appeared. "I'll admit that we weren't always right. This time, though, both Sergeant Guthrie and I think that you might be the only one who can draw out this guy. Make him do something that will reveal his guilt."

"You didn't mention Detective Richards. What does he think?"

"He thinks it's not such a good idea."

"My husband will probably agree with Richards."

A mischievous glint appeared in Morrison's eyes. "I didn't think you had to have your husband's approval for much of anything."

"That's not fair," Tempe said, though she knew Morrison was even more correct than he knew. There were many times she'd gone against Hutch's wishes. "In any case, there is no way I can go to Santa Barbara without Hutch agreeing."

"So ask him."

∾∾

Though she was anxious to tell Hutch about Morrison's request, she drove up to Bear Creek Inn. After parking next to Two John's truck, she entered the kitchen door. Two John sat at a small desk in a corner of the spacious kitchen. He looked up as she entered. None of the kitchen help was around.

"I thought I'd be seeing you sooner than this," he greeted and rose from his place. As usual, two long braids hung down the back of an immaculate white shirt that was tucked into a pair of faded blue jeans. "How was your visit with Vanessa's relative and friends?"

"I had a wonderful time. Vanessa's cousin and her best friend treated me like they'd known me forever. I learned so much about the Tolowa. Unfortunately, I didn't learn anything about who killed Vanessa."

"You probably found out more than you realize," Nick said. "You've sought me out for a reason. What is it?"

How did he do that? "I'm having spirit visitations."

"Vanessa?"

"Yes. She's awakened me two nights in a row."

"What does she want?"

Forcing herself not to display the exasperation she felt, Tempe smiled. "That's what I was hoping you could tell me."

"She didn't speak?"

"Yes, she called me by name. That's how she woke me. I did ask her why she came, but she didn't tell me. She didn't stay long either time."

"What about Hutch? Did he see her too?"

"The first time she appeared he saw something, but I'm not sure he recognized it as Vanessa."

"Why do you think she came to you?"

"I have no idea."

"Sure you do. Think about it."

"Something about her murder, I suppose."

The faintest of smiles lifted Nick's lips. "That's exactly it. She wants your help to bring her murderer to justice."

"What if I can't do that? Is she going to wake me up every night from now on?"

"Bothersome supernatural creatures can be dispersed," Nick said. "However, you have to remember that you are now susceptible to such visits."

Tempe frowned. "What do you mean?"

"Remember, you called back the dead when you wanted to find out what really happened to Doreen Felton. Because you were successful, you created in yourself an easy pathway from the spirit world to you." Nick spoke as though what had happened was a natural turn of events.

"You never warned me about that when you told me how to do it," Tempe said.

"You didn't ask about any side effects."

That comment made Tempe laugh. "Side effects. I never thought there might be such a thing." She sighed. "Are you saying I should expect regular visits from people who have passed on?"

"Only if they need your services."

"If that's what it's all about, then I guess that tells me what I have to do."

"Have to do about what?"

"Detective Morrison wants me to go to Santa Barbara and see Acton Ainsworth. Maybe find out something from him."

Nick's eyes narrowed as he studied Tempe. "There's a lot more that you aren't telling me."

"You're right.. I was followed in Crescent City. Then yesterday, someone butchered a pet pig and put its heart on my front step."

Nick's straight black eyebrows nearly came together as he frowned. "You are in considerable danger."

"You're not the first one who has said that."

"The only way to resolve the issue is to confront it."

"I agree. That's why I'm going to Santa Barbara."

"What does Hutch say?"

"He doesn't know yet. I'm going home to tell him now."

Nick stared at her in his unnerving way, his expression unchanging.

Tempe smiled, "Thanks, Nick. Though I don't know exactly how, you've made me see things clearer."

❧ ❧

As Tempe drove around the corner to the cottage, she spotted Hutch mowing the lawn. She had no idea how he'd react to Detective's Morrison's request. In fact, she was having difficulty digesting the fact that Morrison even suggested such an idea to her. The whole meeting with Morrison had a surrealistic quality to it.

When she parked and opened the door, Hutch hurried toward her with an expectant expression on his face.

"Hey, sweetie. Glad you're home. What did Detective Morrison want?"

"Let's go inside. What I have to tell you is rather bizarre."

"I made some lemonade," Hutch said.

"Sounds good."

Hutch poured two glasses of lemonade, put them on the table and sat opposite her. He waited.

Tempe smiled. "Morrison opened up to me. His father was a highway patrolman killed in the line of duty when Morrison was a teenager. He told me how hard it was for his mother raising her family by herself. She died of cancer last year."

"That's a shame. I'm surprised he decided to tell you all that. It's not like him to open up to you, is it?"

"In a way it made me feel guilty. I've judged both Morrison and Richards without really knowing much about them. I've always been irritated by how they've treated me. Like I didn't know anything. Not capable of helping them with an investigation…unless it somehow involved Indians."

Hutch took hold of her hand. "Don't you think he might have been manipulating you?"

"Oh, I'm sure of it, but I am guilty of exactly what I judged him of doing."

"No doubt that's how he wanted you to feel in order to get you to do whatever it is that he wanted. Which is what?" Hutch ran his free hand through his mussed hair.

Might as well come straight out with it. "Morrison wants me to go to Santa Barbara."

"Why?"

"He has the idea that if I go to Ainsworth's Furniture Store in Santa Barbara, whoever was following me around in Crescent City will make an appearance. If I can draw him out, maybe I can learn something that might be helpful to solving the case."

Hutch's brow furrowed. "What about the pig's heart on the doorstep? What did he think that was about?"

"He thinks it's a warning."

"Me too. So despite that, he thinks you ought to offer yourself as a target?" His voice had a tinge of anger in it.

"He didn't say it quite like that," Tempe said.

"But that's what you'd be." He stared down at his hand holding hers for a long moment. "I suppose you want to do this."

"Frankly, I don't think it will do any good, but yes, I'd like to do it. After spending so much time with Vanessa's cousin and friend, I feel I ought to do what I can to help catch the killer."

"I knew you were going to say that. When are you supposed to go?"

"Right away."

"I know I can't talk you out of doing this, so I'm going with you."

"I'd like that." Tempe leaned over the table and kissed Hutch. "I'll call Sergeant Guthrie and let him know we're both going. Then we can pack. I've never been to Santa Barbara, have you?"

# CHAPTER 24

Before leaving town, Hutch called a deacon to take care of the church and any problems that might occur during his absence. He and Tempe decided to drive to the coast in his new truck. When Tempe put her service revolver in her purse, Hutch asked, "Do you really need to do that?"

"We've had this conversation before. You know that I'm supposed to have my gun with me at all times."

"You've told me often enough, but I'd feel more comfortable if you locked it in the glove compartment of the truck."

"I can do that. However, you need to realize there may come a time when I'll need to have it handy," Tempe said, expecting a lecture on the evils of firearms, one she'd heard before.

When they were first married, Hutch was shocked when he saw her put her revolver in her purse when they were getting ready to go to church. At the time, he'd said, "You aren't going to need that this morning."

She'd explained to him that as a sworn peace officer she was supposed to always have her gun.

He'd argued, "There is no reason for you to have it in church."

She'd quickly cited the case of the man who'd come into a church and shot and killed several people attending the service, including the son of a police officer who didn't have his gun. In fact, there had been other police officers in attendance and no one had a gun with him.

Hutch had told her he didn't think anything like that would ever happen in his little church.

"You never know," Tempe said. "Besides, I'd be willing to bet that nearly everyone in the congregation owns a gun of some kind."

He'd conceded that she was probably right and he hadn't said anymore.

This time he surprised her and didn't launch into his anti-gun argument. Instead, he grinned and said, "I understand."

They made a stop at the sub-station in Dennison to talk to Sergeant Guthrie.

"Come in with me," Tempe said.

"Sure." Hutch raised an eyebrow. "If you want me to."

Guthrie invited them both to sit down in his small office. He didn't seem the least bit surprised to see Hutch and greeted him warmly. To Tempe, he said, "Morrison says you're willing to go to Santa Barbara and poke around."

"Yes, but I'm taking Hutch with me."

"Seems like a good idea to me."

"Glad you think so," Tempe said. Whether Guthrie had agreed or not, Hutch was determined to accompany her. She knew he couldn't be talked out of it.

Guthrie leaned back in his chair, hands behind his head. "Your trip isn't sanctioned by the department."

"Okay," Tempe said.

"If you get in trouble, you're going to have to get out of it on your own." Guthrie glanced at Hutch as though he expected an argument from him.

"I understand. Hopefully, I won't get into trouble."

"That doesn't mean you can't call and ask me for advice. Same thing with Morrison. Just remember, you aren't on official business." Guthrie moved forward, reached into the top drawer of his desk. He pulled out a business size envelope and shoved it towards Tempe.

"What's this?" she asked.

"It's the money you didn't spend while you were in Crescent City. I didn't log it back in. Use it on this trip."

Surprised, Tempe smiled. "Thanks." She tucked the envelope into her purse. "Whose idea was it that I do this? Yours or Morrison?"

Guthrie tipped his head, and bestowed a lop-sided smile on Tempe. "Does it matter?"

"I guess not, but I can't help being curious."

"Actually, Morrison brought it up first. Whether or not you realize it, he admires you."

"He has a funny way of showing it."

Hutch touched Tempe's ankle with the tip of his shoe. She guessed he thought she was being rude.

"Morrison, Richards and I were discussing the case. The detectives had just about decided we'd reached an impasse, that our chances of solving the case were slipping away. Morrison suggested that since you'd been followed in Crescent City, perhaps you'd be willing to nose around in Santa Barbara, see if you could stir something up. Richards didn't think it was such a good idea. But, when that pig heart turned up on your door step, Morrison decided that your appearance in Santa Barbara was the only hope that we might get something on the victim's husband."

"Did either of you talk about what I ought to do when I get to Santa Barbara? After all, it is a good-sized city. How is Acton Ainsworth even going to know I'm there?" Actually Tempe already had a plan in mind, but she wanted to hear if Sergeant Guthrie and Morrison had come up with the same.

"Go to the furniture store, of course. See if you can find out where his main office is. Get an appointment and see if he'll talk to you about his wife and her murder," Guthrie said.

Tempe nodded. "That was more or less my plan."

Staring at her, Hutch knitted his brow. "It was? That sounds kind of dangerous."

"I'm not worried. You're going to be with me, remember?"

❧❧

The trip through Bakersfield to Highway 5 through the

Angeles National Forest was crowded, as usual, but uneventful. Tempe and Hutch had plenty of time to discuss their coming adventure.

At one point, Hutch asked, "Do you even know where the furniture store we're supposed to go to is located?"

Tempe had been wondering the same thing. "Not exactly, but I'm sure we can ask someone or look in the phone book."

"Do you really think it'll do any good? If this man is responsible for his wife's murder he's been extremely good at covering his tracks. I wouldn't think you turning up in his territory is going to shake him enough to confess."

"I don't think anyone expects him to do that."

"What do they expect?"

"That seeing me will trigger something."

Hutch sighed. "Trigger something. That's what worries me. You're making yourself an irresistible target."

Tempe laughed. "I guess trigger wasn't the best word to use in this instance."

"Actually this whole trip seems futile to me."

"Maybe, but you're forgetting about the man who followed me around in Crescent City. There's a pretty good chance that he's Acton Ainsworth's employee."

"Yes. He might even be the one who killed Vanessa. If that's so, when you turn up in Ainsworth's store, you'll be that target you've talked about."

"That's probably what Morrison is hoping for. He wants Ainsworth to do something to reveal his part in his wife's murder."

"Why do you think he even sent someone after you when you went to Crescent City?" Hutch asked. "The investigation would have ended right there when you didn't find out anything helpful from Vanessa's cousin or her friend."

"According to Abby, Acton is paranoid. That could mean he's worried about someone finding out what he's done. Whether or not he knew I was going to Crescent City, I don't know. Maybe he just sent someone up there to nose around the same time I happened to be there."

"Or maybe whoever this guy is, he was keeping an eye on you in Bear Creek," Hutch suggested.

"Could be, but I sure didn't notice anyone new in town. Then again, I wasn't watching for anyone." The sign for the turn off for 126 came into view. "That's where we get off."

They drove past orange groves, a fish hatchery, tree farms and through the growing towns of Fillmore and Santa Paula, and kept going until they reached Highway 101 where the traffic immediately increased. They passed through Ventura, where the vista opened up to the ocean on the left and the hills to the right. Obviously, everyone else on the road was used to the gorgeous panorama as they sped toward or away from Santa Barbara at speeds ten and twenty miles over the limit. They passed the beach at Rincon where motor homes were parked nose-to-nose along the ocean front.

"Oh my goodness, look at that," Tempe said, peering out her passenger window. "That's where they had that terrible mudslide that buried all those houses. Looks like people are still living there." A huge part of the hillside had slid to a stop against more homes.

Their conversation changed to other matters: when Blair might come and visit again, people at church and their problems, and remodeling they might do to their cottage.

When they reached Carpenteria, the colors and landscape began to change. The mountains on the right were farther from the freeway. Hutch asked, "I forgot to ask you what you found out from Nick Two John about Vanessa's spirit."

"You know how Nick is. He didn't seem the least bit surprised. He did wonder if you'd seen her too."

Shrugging, Hutch said, "I saw something. I'm not sure what though."

"He thinks I'm more susceptible to spirits now."

"I'm not surprised." His hands tightened on the steering wheel.

"He said that Vanessa wants me to find out who killed her."

"Doesn't she know?"

Sometimes Hutch's remarks made her laugh. This was one of those times.

He frowned at her. "What's funny about that?"

"Of course Vanessa knows, she just wants her murderer brought to justice."

"I guess that is pretty obvious." He glanced at her with a half smile. "Did he have any other wise words for you?"

Tempe considered a moment before answering truthfully. "He thinks I'm in danger."

"There's enough of us who believe that to form a club," Hutch said.

They came over a rise where the trees from the hills met the ocean. Montecito.

"I've heard this is where a lot of movie stars live," Tempe said.

On the left was a hotel that had obviously seen better days and then they passed an industrial section and almost immediately came into downtown Santa Barbara. The highway divided the city with the beach on one side and the city and the mountains on the other.

"So where do we go now?"

# CHAPTER 25

Hutch drove up and down streets in the older part of Santa Barbara so Tempe could watch for a suitable motel or hotel to use as a base. Most looked far too expensive, especially the ones anywhere near the beach.

"We could make this into a bit of a vacation," Hutch said. "Squeeze in some of sightseeing while dangling you as bait." He turned off State Street that meandered through what looked like the old part of Santa Barbara, lined with intriguing shops and restaurants, all with red-tile roofs.

"Oh, Hutch, slow down." Tempe pointed at an old Victorian house with turrets and unusual windows, scrolls and trim painted in various shades of pink, burgundy, and violet. Noticeable because it was the only building that she'd seen that wasn't white stucco with the signature red tile roof. A sign in front said, "The Gingerbread House Bed and Breakfast."

"Let's see if they have a room," she said.

Hutch drive around the corner into the guest parking lot. "It's probably way out of our budget range."

"If it's more than we have in this envelope, we'll bill it to the department."

"Good idea." He parked the truck beside a Lexus.

Confidently, Hutch followed behind Tempe carrying their overnight bags as she headed toward the front steps. Inside what had once been an entry hall, she found a small desk with a bell. A grand staircase led to the second floor. She could see through closed beveled glass doors a formal dining room on one side and a sitting room or parlor on the other, both with old fashioned charm.

A gray haired, thin woman in jeans and open white shirt over a bright red T-shirt, clumped down the stairs barefooted. When she reached the bottom, she frowned at Tempe and Hutch. "May I help you?"

"We're hoping you might have a room," Tempe said quickly.

"You didn't make a reservation?" the woman asked.

Tempe smiled. "We didn't know we were coming to Santa Barbara until this morning. I fell in love with this inn the minute I saw it."

"Are you here on business?" The woman frowned as though suspicious.

Hutch set down the bags and held his hand out to her. "I'm Pastor Hutchinson from Bear Creek. This is my wife Tempe."

The woman's face softened and she shook Hutch's offered hand. "I'm Denise, the owner. You're in luck. I've had an unexpected cancellation for two nights. How long did you plan to stay?"

Tempe lifted her eyebrows in Hutch's direction.

"Two nights will be perfect," he said.

Denise stepped behind the small desk, opened a guest book and turned it around toward Hutch. "Just sign your name and address here." She pulled out a brochure and handed it to him. "The room in question is called 'The Rose Suite.' All our rooms have flower names."

She pointed to the room on the open brochure. Tempe peeked around Hutch at the price. Her expression must have revealed her shock because Denise quickly said, "Since we have a non-refundable policy for the reservation payment, I can let you have the room for half-price."

"That would be wonderful." Tempe handed Hutch the envelope with the money.

He counted out the bills and gave them to Denise.

She tipped her head and stared at the money in her hand.

"Almost everyone pays with a credit card."

"Is it a problem to use cash?" Hutch asked.

"Goodness, no. Bring your bags with you and I'll take you to your room. We're having hors d'oeuvres and wine in the dining room starting in about a half hour. When you come down I'll give you your receipt."

❦

After Denise left them, Hutch said, "No wonder it's called the Rose Room."

The wallpaper was splashed with faded cabbage roses interspersed with stripes. The mahogany four poster bed had a duvet printed in similar pink and red roses. Pillows in various pink and red prints were heaped on the bed. Matching bedside tables and lamps were also heavily decorated with pink and red roses. Two antique armoires balanced the room. The floors were worn but shiny hardwood.

"Look at this." Tempe opened the door to the bathroom. Inside, a claw-foot bathtub sat on a platform with steps. A pink-and-white striped shower curtain hung from a circular rod. White tile covered the floor and walls. A free-standing sink had towel racks on either side that held fluffy pink and white towels. The toilet had an overhead tank with a pull-chain on it.

Hutch peeked out the one window of the bedroom. "Not a great view, but not bad either."

Tempe joined him and peered out at an old-fashioned flower garden with a fountain and gazebo. The parking lot was not quite hidden by the trees and trellises. "Let's get unpacked. I'm starving."

"Me too."

They took advantage of the Gingerbread Inn's food offerings. None of the other guests made an appearance, so they had first choice of the wonderful cheeses and cold cuts, crackers and dips, sliced apples and pears, and some chunky Chocolate Chip cookies. Though the wines all had French labels, Tempe decided drinking sparkling soda would be the smarter choice since they had no idea what a confrontation with Acton Ainsworth might bring.

Denise came into the room and handed them their receipt. "We're close enough to walk to the Santa Barbara Mission. It's a little farther to the beach, and I'm sure you noticed that we're very close to Santa Barbara's main shopping area."

"Perhaps you can tell us how to get to the Ainsworth Furniture store," Hutch said.

A puzzled expression crossed Denise's face. After a moment, she gave them the directions.

When they were in the truck, driving toward their destination, Tempe said, "I'm sure our hostess wondered why on earth we wanted to go to a furniture store."

"It was obvious she thought it an odd request since we live out of town. I hope we have time to look around a bit before we head home. I'd love to see the mission," Hutch said.

"It'll all depends on how things go."

They followed the 101 north until they came to the street Denise had told them to watch for. They discovered what looked like a new shopping center with all the usual stores, but the architecture was the old-mission style with red tile roofs. Ainsworth Elegant Furniture was the largest and held a corner spot.

Hutch found a parking place not far from the entrance. "I'm coming with you."

"Fine with me. If I'm able to get in to see Mr. Ainsworth, perhaps you can look around and see if you can spot a partially bald man, medium height, a bit overweight. Could have on a baseball hat, maybe a leather jacket."

"Oh sure." Hutch laughed. "The mysterious stranger who followed you. That's a pretty vague description."

"The first time I saw him he had a mustache, but that seems to come and go."

"Do you think he'll recognize you?"

"If he's around, he'll recognize me all right."

Automatic glass doors opened into a vast interior with furniture in tasteful groupings in different room styles. Tempe glanced around, but before she could decide where to go, a tall man wearing a dark suit and tie approached them.

"May I help you?" he asked.

Taken by surprise, Tempe said, "I'd like to see Mr. Acton Ainsworth."

The man frowned. "Is there a problem? Perhaps I can be of some assistance."

"Thank you, but no. This is personal."

"I don't think Mr. Acton is here. He has an office here, but it's not the main one. You might go back there," the tall salesman pointed toward the rear of the store. "Give your name to his assistant. She should be able to arrange an appointment for you." The tall salesman pointed toward the rear of the building.

"Thank you."

Hutch nodded to the man and followed Tempe. When they were out of hearing range, in a low voice Hutch said, "I'll come back there with you, just in case that other guy is hanging around."

Once they'd wound their way through all the sofas and chairs, dining room tables and glass fronted buffets and fancy bedroom suites, they found a door with a brass sign stating it was the office. Tempe opened the door and they stepped inside.

A blonde wearing too much eye make-up glanced from a computer monitor. "Oh."

"Hi," Tempe said. "We're looking for Mr. Ainsworth. Is he here?"

"No."

"Can you tell me where we can find him? It's important." Tempe judged the woman to be middle-aged despite her efforts to look younger.

"Umm, well, I can call him and set up an appointment. Your name is?"

Tempe pulled her wallet from her purse and opened it to her identification. "I'm Deputy Crabtree."

The black outlined eyes with the artificial lashes loaded

with mascara opened wide. "Oh, my. Is this official business?"

"I'd like to speak with Mr. Ainsworth concerning his wife's death."

The woman turned to her telephone and dialed. She asked for Ainsworth and obviously was given another number which she punched in. After a few moments, she said, "Sir, I'm sorry to bother you at home, but a Deputy Crabtree is here at the store and would like to have a word with you."

She handed the receiver to Tempe.

"Hello, Mr. Ainsworth. I'd like to meet with you as soon as possible," Tempe said.

Ainsworth's voice was deep and well-modulated. "I'm so sorry. You should have called for an appointment. I'm unavailable this evening. I might be able to squeeze you in sometime tomorrow. Where can I get in touch with you?"

Putting her hand over the mouthpiece of the phone, Tempe turned to Hutch. "Do you have the number of the Inn?"

Hutch pulled a card out of his pocket and handed it to her.

"I'm staying at the Gingerbread Inn," she read the phone number, "under the name of Hutchinson. If we aren't there when you call, leave a message, please."

"I'll call you later this evening. Please put my assistant back on the line."

Tempe handed over the phone. "He wants to talk to you again." She waited in case he gave the assistant instructions pertaining to her appointment, but the woman dismissed her with a wave.

As they left the office, the assistant said, "Yes, sir, I'll contact him right away."

# CHAPTER 26

Back in the truck, Hutch asked, "Who do you think Mr. Ainsworth wanted his assistant to contact?"

"I'm guessing it's the same man who followed me in Crescent City."

"So what do you want to do now?" Hutch glanced at his watch. "It's still fairly early."

"Why don't we go to the ocean and look around down there while it's still light. I doubt if Ainsworth will call me anytime soon, if at all. I may have to track him down some other way."

"I agree. Then let's find a nice place for dinner before we head back to the Gingerbread House," Hutch said.

"In the morning, if we haven't heard from Ainsworth, I'll see if I can find out where he lives."

"I'd like to fit in a walk to the mission if there's time." Hutch turned his truck into a public parking lot along the beachfront.

❧❧

It was difficult to think about trying to catch a murderer while watching a colorful sunset fade over the ocean. They enjoyed a delicious seafood dinner. Feeling content and comfortable, Tempe and Hutch returned to the bed and breakfast. They stepped inside the parlor where a large group gathered. They wanted to let Denise know they were back for the evening.

The thin woman had changed into a long black skirt and

turtleneck sweater with a clunky, silver necklace that nearly reached her waist. "Oh, the Hutchinsons. You've had several phone calls." She plucked some yellow notes from the pocket of her skirt and brought them to Hutch. "Join us. Say hello to your fellow guests."

Tempe glanced around. Curious faces peered at them. Anxious to see the phone messages, she wasn't interested in meeting new people and chatting idly.

Obviously, Hutch had other ideas. He stuffed the yellow notes into his pocket, moved toward the first couple sitting on an old- fashioned velvet settee. "Hi, I'm Hutch and this is my wife, Tempe."

She was glad he didn't identify himself as a preacher or her as a deputy since she knew that would increase the chance for unwanted questions. They moved from couple to couple and met Dr. and Mrs. Bucklin, a retired physician and his wife, both portly, from somewhere in Illinois. A pair in their early sixties explained they owned and operated a home for the developmentally disabled in Fresno and were vacationing at the same time their clients took a chaperoned cruise to Mexico. A gay couple introduced themselves as life-partners; handsome men dressed casually in faded Levis, collared knit-shirts and sport coats. A young couple who held hands announced that they were on their honeymoon. Everyone had a glass of wine either in his or her hand or on a nearby table.

Once they'd made the rounds shaking hands, and before Hutch could make himself comfortable, Tempe said, "It's nice to meet you all, but we've had an extremely long day and I'm anxious to try out that bed upstairs."

The newly-weds giggled. Everyone murmured appropriate remarks. Hutch frowned, obviously disappointed not to have the opportunity to socialize. Tempe tucked her arm in the crook of his elbow and urged him toward the doorway.

Once they closed the glass doors behind them, Hutch said, "We could have been a bit sociable."

"Honey, we don't have much time left." Tempe galloped up the stairs ahead of Hutch, unlocked the door to their room and went inside.

Before Hutch was all the way in, Tempe said, "Quick, hand them over."

Dutifully, he plucked the notes from his pocket and held them out to her. "Darn, I thought you meant what you said about the bed."

"Later." Tempe stared at the notes in her hand. Fortunately, Denise, or whoever took the messages, not only put the dates down, but also the times the messages were received. The first one came in while Tempe and Hutch strolled along the beach. The second and third while they were enjoying their dinner and coffee afterwards. The fourth just before they arrived at The Gingerbread House. Every message was the same, call Acton Ainsworth ASAP, with various telephone numbers.

Moving to the French telephone on the night stand, Tempe dialed the latest number.

A female voice with a thick Hispanic accent answered. "Ainsworth residence. Who is calling please?"

"This is Deputy Crabtree calling for Mr. Ainsworth."

"Mr. Ainsworth, he say when you call to tell you he meet with you tomorrow at his mountain home."

"Did he say what time?"

"Yes, he say one o'clock in the afternoon."

"And, may I have the address, please?"

She gave an address that sounded like it was someplace away from Santa Barbara. Tempe wrote it down. "Did he leave any directions as to how to find it?"

"It is close to San Marcos Pass. That is not where I work."

"Tell Mr. Ainsworth we'll be there. Thank you." Tempe replaced the receiver.

"We'll be where?" Hutch asked.

"Mr. Ainsworth's mountain home."

"Where is that?"

"I'm not sure. The person I was talking to said it's off San Marcos Pass."

"How will we find it?"

"I'll see if I can borrow Denise's computer in the morning and get driving directions that way. Denise might even have some suggestions."

"Sounds like we should have time to visit the mission," Hutch said.

"I'm sure we will." Tempe hugged Hutch and lifted her face for a kiss. "Are you up for trying out the tub?"

⁓⁓

"Tempe."

Tempe opened her eyes and for a moment had no idea where she was.

"Tempe." That now familiar voice was even more insistent.

Sitting up, Tempe could see the silvery outline of what she knew was the essence of Vanessa Ainsworth. Though she couldn't see much of anything else in the darkness of the room, Vanessa's spirit was plainly visible, shimmering and luminous.

"Yes, Vanessa, I'm here now. I'm going to see Acton."

The wispy form shivered violently.

"I'll do my best to find out something that proves he caused your death."

Vanessa's face contorted, her mouth forming another word. "Danger." She faded into the darkness.

Tempe didn't need a ghost to tell her she was in danger. She hoped she could go back to sleep after being so abruptly awakened. At least Hutch had slept through the visitation.

⁓⁓

Fortunately, despite the eerie nighttime disturbance, Tempe fell asleep again. She was awakened by Hutch pulling open the curtains.

"It's foggy," Hutch said. "Hopefully it'll burn off before too long. How are you this morning?"

Tempe stretched. "Great."

He leaned down and kissed her. "Me too. I'm starving."

Breakfast was served in the formal dining room. Denise informed them they were the first to come downstairs. Crystal champagne glasses were arranged on the sideboard alongside silver tubs filled with ice holding glass pitchers with a variety of juices.

"Help yourselves to the juice. Sit wherever you'd like. I'll have your breakfast ready in a moment."

Breakfast consisted of a choice of home baked breads, popovers, fresh fruit, crispy bacon and sausage patties, along with the best scrambled eggs Tempe had ever tasted. Everything was served on beautiful China. Denise kept the coffee cups filled.

While pouring seconds, Denise asked, "What are your plans for today?"

"We're going to the mission this morning," Hutch said.

"This afternoon we're visiting a friend who lives somewhere off the San Marcos Pass. We have his address but no directions. I was wondering, may I use your computer?"

Denise smiled. "Give me the address and I'll find the directions for you while you're finishing your breakfast."

"That would be great." Tempe handed her the address she'd copied down.

When Denise returned with the folded computer papers, she said, "You better get a fairly early start. The highway isn't bad, and the scenery is great. I have no idea what condition the road will be in after you turn off. The directions are pretty straight-forward. You shouldn't have any trouble finding it. It won't be foggy up there." After handing over the directions, Denise poured herself a cup of coffee and sat across from them. "Do you know anything about the San Marcos Pass Road?"

"Afraid not," Hutch said.

"What's interesting is that the area around the pass was first inhabited by the Chumash. It once was a stage route. The pass is a shortcut through the mountains that will take you over the Santa Ynez Mountains and back onto Highway 101, 35 miles inland. If you have time, you might want to go all the way and visit Solvang. The views both ways are spectacular."

She might have told them more, but the plump doctor

and his wife appeared at the glass door and she jumped to her feet to greet them.

Hutch and Tempe chit-chatted for a few minutes with the other guests before excusing themselves.

"Do you want to walk to the mission?" Hutch asked. "Denise says it takes less than twenty minutes."

"Might be a good idea to walk off some of that delicious breakfast."

The fog had nearly disappeared by the time they strolled toward the mission. As they headed up Laguna Street, they could see a cross and the white mission and its bell towers. "Wow, that's impressive," Hutch said.

"I remember studying all the California missions in grammar school." Tempe glanced one way, then the other before stepping off the curb to cross the street.

"We had to make a model of a mission. Mine was the one in San Luis Obispo."

The sound of a racing engine drew Tempe's attention. "Oh, my Lord, Hutch, watch out!"

A huge, black SUV bore down on them.

# CHAPTER 27

Both leapt back on the sidewalk, but the SUV kept coming. It looked like it was going to jump the curb. Tempe's heart pounded so hard, it hurt her ears.

Hutch grabbed her around the waist and shoved her ahead of him, towards a short, cement wall surrounding the front lawn of a small stucco house. Tempe stumbled and fell headlong on the grass. Hutch landed on his knees beside her.

The SUV roared past, speeding up the street toward the mission.

"Are you all right?" Hutch helped Tempe to her feet. "What was wrong that guy? Do you think he was drunk this early in the morning?"

"No, I think that was the man who followed me in Crescent City." Tempe brushed at the grass stuck on her knees.

"Could you see his face?"

"No, but that was deliberate. Whoever was driving meant to hit us."

"This is far more serious than I thought," Hutch said. "What do we do now?"

"Under ordinary circumstances, I'd call the police. But all we know is that it was a black SUV. Do you know what kind?"

Hutch shrugged. "Not really, just one of the big ones. A Suburban maybe or an Escalade. I don't know."

"Neither of us saw the license number, so there's nothing for the police to go on."

"Should we go back?" Hutch asked.

"We're almost at the mission. He probably won't try that again. He'll know we're watching for him," Tempe said. "When we get back, I'll give Sergeant Guthrie a call and let him know what happened."

Though the mission was beautiful and steeped in history, Tempe couldn't enjoy it fully. Her mind was too full of the danger she was subjecting herself and Hutch, in this attempt to get Acton Ainsworth to reveal himself as his wife's murderer.

While wandering through the old, beautiful structure, Hutch read facts from a brochure he'd picked up at the entrance. "'The Chumash lived here before the Spanish arrived'," he said.

"Um huh." Another Indian tribe she didn't know anything about. Tempe knew Hutch was valiantly attempting to distract her from what had just happened.

"'The Franciscan monks introduced agriculture to the Indians. Water was brought down from the mountain creeks to irrigate the fields and for domestic use.'" Hutch continued his reading. "'They built a dam and the water flowed to the mission by an aqueduct'."

Though Tempe heard the words, her mind was busy thinking about how they could best protect themselves—especially when they ventured into the mountains to meet Ainsworth. Her service revolver was still locked up in the glove compartment of Hutch's truck.

Hutch didn't seem to notice her inattention or if he did, he still hoped to interest her in what he was telling her. "'The Indians made adobes, tiles, shoes and woolen garments. They learned how to do carpentry and masonry.' Oh, this is interesting, they also learned how to sing and play European music and instruments, violins, cellos, and horns. 'The main purpose of the mission was to make Christians out of the Chumash.'"

"It sounds like they accomplished their goal." Tempe followed Hutch as he went from room to room, continuing to read as he went along.

"Here's something I didn't know. 'The Governor of California confiscated the lands and sold the mission. The missionaries were allowed to continue conducting services in the sanctuary. Abraham Lincoln returned the Mission to the Catholic Church in 1865'."

She could feel the aura of history surrounding her. In fact, there was more, it was as though there was someone or something beyond her peripheral vision attempting to gain her attention. Quickly, she turned her head, but no one was there. If she concentrated more perhaps she could bring whoever it was into view, but her mind was in the future, not the past. Glancing at her watch, she said, "I think we ought to be getting back. We don't know how long it's going to take us to find Ainsworth's home."

Disappointment shadowed Hutch's face. "You're probably right."

Walking back to the bed-and-breakfast, both Tempe and Hutch paid a lot of attention to their surroundings, particularly cars as they passed. However, on the return trip, no vehicle threatened them as they crossed streets.

"Maybe whoever almost struck us had nothing to do with your stalker," Hutch offered.

"That's possible," Tempe said, but knew in her heart that wasn't so.

Back in their room, Tempe called Sergeant Guthrie. "I just wanted you to know that we're meeting with Acton Ainsworth at one this afternoon. Just in case, here's his address." She gave it to him. "It's somewhere off San Marcos Pass."

"Sounds like it's in the mountains," the sergeant said.

"Yes, but not like our mountains."

"I'm not sure what that means."

Tempe laughed, "Me either. I have to tell you what happened this morning." She described almost getting hit by the speeding car.

"But you don't know for sure if it was the same driver

who followed you in Crescent City, right?"

"No. I was too busy getting out of the way to look at the driver."

Guthrie didn't say anything for such a long time, Tempe wondered if they'd been cut off.

"This plan may be too dangerous for you to continue. How do you feel about it?"

"We've come this far. I don't want to quit now."

"We really have no assurance that Ainsworth will do or say anything that will prove a connection to his wife's murder."

"I've thought about that, but I want to try," Tempe said. Besides if she didn't, no telling how long Vanessa would continue her visitations.

"Okay, but if you feel like you're threatened in any way, get out of there."

"Don't worry, I will."

When she hung up, Hutch shrugged into a corduroy jacket. "Sounds like we're still going to visit Mr. Ainsworth."

Tempe nodded.

❦

Following the gently curving two-lane highway, the view consisted of gentle slopes, deep canyons, grasslands and live oak trees. Tempe read a print-out of the computer directions to Hutch as they drove upward. They came to a sign alerting them to the fact that the Lake Cachuma turnoff was coming soon.

"Okay, now watch carefully. Deer Creek Lane is supposed to be off to the left."

"I see it," Hutch said, slowing and maneuvering into a turning lane. He drove across the highway and entered a narrow, paved road.

The foliage thickened. Manzanita and scrub brush crowded in among the spindly trunks of pine trees and the thick trunks of live oaks. As they drove slowly, breaks in the foliage indicated roads off to each side, marked with a lone mail box or several on a shelf supported by one long post.

Tempe read off the numbers she could see. "We've a way to go, I think."

Once in awhile, they'd catch a glimpse of a house or cabin off in the distance. The farther they drove, the larger the dwellings and more distance between each one. Tempe opened her window and took a deep breath. The air smelled fresh and clean, laced with the scent of pine. It also was warmer up here than it had been down near the ocean.

Up ahead, Tempe spotted a fancy mailbox off to the left. It had been built to look like a Spanish-style house, with a roof that resembled red tile. "Slow down, I think we're coming to the right driveway."

Sure enough, the front of the small mailbox house had the numbers that belonged to Acton Ainsworth's residence. Hutch turned in. Surprisingly, the drive was wide and covered with gravel. It curved and rose higher and higher until they reached a paved driveway lined with sculptured conifers and other evergreens that circled in front of a large, sprawling, one story white stucco home, with the requisite red tiled roof, and an attached four-door garage. A shiny red Porsche was parked in front of the wide, marble steps that led to the double front door. Stained glass windows adorned each one.

"Impressive," Tempe said. "The furniture business must be doing very well."

"I'm glad I have my new truck. They might not have allowed me to park my old one near the Porsche."

Glancing at her watch, Tempe said, "We're right on time." She reached for the glove compartment.

Hutch frowned. "You aren't going to need your gun here, are you?"

"I certainly hope not, but I need to be prepared. After all, it's quite likely that Ainsworth planned his wife's murder." Tempe used her key to unlock the glove compartment. She removed the revolver and slid it into her purse, which she tucked under her arm.

They hadn't quite reached the front door when it opened.

A tall man, very tan, a full head of sandy-colored hair, stepped out and greeted them with a big smile filled with gleaming white, perfect teeth. Acton Ainsworth looked very much like the photograph Tempe had seen in the newspaper. The difference was that in person she could see that he'd obviously had some plastic surgery. His straight nose was just a bit too perfect. Despite the sun-darkened skin, his face had few lines. His eyes had a surprised quality to them, though the color was so dark Tempe couldn't see where his pupils began. She couldn't decide if his hair was real, but the color certainly wasn't. He wore a golfing shirt and white pants. Though Tempe guessed he was probably in his mid to late fifties, he certainly worked hard at appearing much younger.

Before he could say anything, Tempe strode up the stairs with her hand outstretched. "Hi, I'm Deputy Tempe Crabtree, Tulare County Sheriff's Department."

He studied her for a brief moment, before giving her hand a quick shake. "I'm sure you already know who I am. And who is this?" He moved his head toward Hutch.

Hutch stepped up next to Tempe and shook Ainsworth's hand. "Hutch Hutchinson."

A quizzical expression crossed Ainsworth's face. "Nice to meet you." It didn't sound as though he meant it. He returned his attention to Tempe. "I expected you to be in uniform."

"I'm not here on official business," Tempe said.

"Really. Are you saying this is a social visit?" Ainsworth crossed his arms.

Tempe smiled. "In a way. We're from Bear Creek. My husband and I both knew Vanessa."

Hutch stared at her. She knew he was thinking she wasn't being exactly truthful.

Finally, he opened the front door wider and stepped aside to allow them entrance.

"I have no idea why you would want to talk to me, but since you came all this way it wouldn't be hospitable on my part not to invite you in."

The enormous entry hall floor was shiny marble with a

pinkish tinge. A huge mirror hung on one side, reflecting a coat of arms embroidered on a hanging on the opposite wall. Suspended from the ceiling was a multi-faceted crystal chandelier. The entry hall opened onto a huge living room with floor to ceiling windows and a set of French doors.

"Come in and take a seat," Ainsworth said, in a cold voice.

Tempe didn't quite know where to go. There were at least five seating groups complete with soft-leather and beautiful fabric couches, chairs and low tables. Except for the fact it wasn't as crowded, it reminded Tempe of the man's furniture store showroom. The drape-less windows beckoned to her. She was eager to see the view. Without invitation, she crossed the bare, highly polished plank floor and an occasional Persian rug until she reached the expanse of glass.

"Oh, my," she gasped. Before her lay a flagstone patio, a huge irregularly shaped pool with a waterfall at one end, and beyond that the view spread over the canyons all the way to the ocean. White clouds scattered across the sky overhead. "This is absolutely beautiful." She turned back toward Ainsworth and her husband.

"I agree," Ainsworth said. He moved closer and so did Hutch.

Tempe smiled. It looked like Hutch was following Ainsworth to keep an eye on him.

Ainsworth crossed his arms and stared at Tempe. "What is it exactly that brought you to see me? Not to admire the vista from my living room, I'm sure."

The contrast between the glowering Ainsworth and the beauty of his elegant possessions only surpassed by the splendor of nature on display was not lost on Tempe.

She eased herself into the nearest chair. One that was so big and soft, she felt enveloped by it. For a moment, the comfort made her forget her purpose.

Ainsworth continued to stare at her with menace in his eyes, but he did perch himself on the wide arm of a nearby couch. Hutch continued his close watch behind their host.

"I'm here about your wife's murder," Tempe began.

"My ex-wife. I was right here in Santa Barbara at the time of Vanessa's death. Detectives from Tulare County came here to interview me and the Santa Barbara P.D. verified my alibi. I don't understand what more you people could possibly need from me." Ainsworth studied his manicured fingernails. From the condition of his hands, it was obvious he didn't do any manual labor.

"This is quite a place. You must have a large staff to take care of everything," Tempe said.

Tipping his head, without a strand of his sandy hair moving, he stared at Tempe. "I fail to see what business that is of yours, Deputy...Crabtree, is it?"

"Yes, that's my name, Deputy Crabtree. I doubt if you are having any trouble remembering it. After all, you sent your man to Crescent City the same time that I was there visiting Vanessa's cousin and best friend."

Beneath his tan, Ainsworth's face darkened even more. Anger flashed in his eyes. "I have no idea what you're talking about. Anything you learned from that crazy Indian, Abigail Jacoby or her equally crazy friend, Justine, is nothing but hogwash. From the time Vanessa and I first married, they did nothing but try to undermine our relationship."

"That certainly is different from what they told me," Tempe said.

It was obvious Ainsworth was trying to control his anger. His hands shook until he clasped them together on his knees. "Really, and I suppose nothing will stop you from telling me their lies."

"I think you need to be confronted by what I heard. After all, you sent someone to Crescent City who followed me around to find out what I was learning about you," Tempe said, matter-of-factly.

Ainsworth's teeth, which he so often displayed in a dazzling grin, now were exposed in a threatening grimace. "How would I know that you were in Crescent City?"

"I don't think you did know. I think it was a coincidence that I happened to be there at the same time as the man you sent to see if anything was going on with Vanessa's cousin and her friends that might be detrimental to you."

With narrowed eyes, Ainsworth glared at her. "Are you hinting that you did find evidence that connects me to her murder?"

"I learned that you are paranoid. During your marriage to Vanessa you kept her a virtual prisoner. You cut her off from her friends and relatives and you stifled her as an artist, wouldn't let her show her paintings unless you were with her all the time."

"Did you even know Vanessa?" Ainsworth spat at her.

"I didn't know Vanessa well, but I did know she was a very talented woman."

"Not only talented, but attractive to men. I had to protect my marriage." His voice had risen. "You have no idea what it was like for a man like me to be married to a woman as attractive and talented as Vanessa."

"I can guess that it was pretty hard on your ego."

Ainsworth ignored her remark, but said, "No matter where we went, men hovered around her. When she was at an art show, they hung around to compliment her work, but I knew they had ulterior motives. When she went to parties with my friends, the men didn't have the decency to pretend they were interested in her art. They undressed her with their eyes. Their desire to have her as apparent as if they were drooling, and some of them were. If I hadn't always been around, no telling what might have happened."

For the first time, Hutch spoke. "Obviously the most important component of a marriage was lacking in yours."

Startled, Ainsworth swung around and scowled at Hutch. "And what is that?"

"Trust."

"Ha. Trust is something I don't believe in when it comes to a relationship between a man and a woman. What gives you any authority in the matter?"

"I'm a minister and have been doing counseling couples for years. Lack of trust causes more problems in a marriage than anything else."

This information seemed to startle Ainsworth. Obviously, his hired man hadn't done a thorough background check on Tempe. Turning back to her, he said, "This is your husband?"

"Who did you think he was?" Tempe asked.

"I was told two detectives had come to see me."

"Who told you that?"

For a moment Tempe thought he might actually tell her.

He opened his mouth and sputtered. Jumping to his feet, he hollered, "I've had enough of you. Get out of my house! Now!"

"Well Hutch, it's time to go. It sounds like we've worn out our welcome." Tempe smiled at Ainsworth. "You have a beautiful home."

"Out!" Ainsworth shouted, waving his arms wildly.

Hutch put a protective arm around Tempe and escorted her toward the door.

She paused and turned to face Ainsworth again. "I understand you were upset about the alimony Vanessa was awarded when you two divorced."

"She didn't deserve a bit of it," Ainsworth growled.

"Is that why you had her killed, so you wouldn't have to pay her any more money?"

Ainsworth's complexion turned a deep shade of purple. He gasped as though he couldn't breathe.

For a moment, Tempe thought the man might have a stroke. Instead, he leapt toward Tempe.

# CHAPTER 28

Putting his body in front of Tempe, Hutch said, "That's far enough."

Tempe poked her head out from behind her husband. "That could be why Vanessa finally left you."

"And how would you know that?" Ainsworth growled.

"Her cousin told me that you'd been physically abusive."

"Out!" Ainsworth shouted, spraying spittle. "Get out while I'm still in control of myself. Don't come back."

Hutch opened the door and followed Tempe through it. Ainsworth slammed it behind them.

"Well, that was interesting," Hutch said. "You certainly annoyed him. Do you think it will do any good?"

"We didn't get a confession if that's what you mean. We'll have to wait and see what he does next."

Hutch opened the passenger door of his truck. "What do you think that will be?"

Tempe climbed in. "I haven't a clue, but whatever it is won't be nice. But I do have an idea. Let's stop at the library in Santa Barbara. I want to look up a news article." Without waiting for Hutch to ask her to do so, she took her revolver out of her purse and put it back in the glove compartment.

He smiled but made no comment about the gun. "Do you know where the library is?"

"No, but it shouldn't be too hard to find. Probably around the downtown area."

"I don't know if that man is responsible for his wife's

death, but he certainly has problems," Hutch said. "Everything you said to him brought him closer and closer to blowing his top."

"I was hoping he might do just that and say something to incriminate himself."

"For a moment I thought he might hit you."

They continued discussing Ainsworth, his home, and whether or not he'd hired someone to kill his wife.

When they reached the end of the road and were waiting to turn onto the highway, a black Suburban sped in, nearly clipping Hutch's truck.

"What's the matter with that guy?" Hutch said.

Tempe only caught a glimpse of the driver. "Do you think that's the same SUV that tried to run us down this morning?"

"Could be."

"I couldn't see the driver too well, but enough to think that he was the same guy who was following me in Crescent City."

"Do you think Ainsworth already called him to let him know about our visit?"

"I wouldn't doubt it."

"Oh boy. What do you think they'll do now?"

"I have no idea, but we'd better pay attention to what's going on around us."

All the way to Santa Barbara, Tempe kept watch on the highway behind them, expecting the black Suburban to appear at anytime. She wouldn't have been at all surprised if it came along and tried to run to run them off the road.

Having arrived back in town without incident, Hutch said, "Perhaps we're the ones who are paranoid. Suburbans are popular, especially with people who live in the mountains. We certainly know plenty of folks who have them. The one we saw just now might have belonged to someone who lived on the same road as Ainsworth."

"That's possible, but in any case, I'm sure Ainsworth isn't through with us."

They didn't locate the public library, but as they were

driving down one of the streets Tempe spotted the office of the Santa Barbara Daily News. "Turn into that parking lot. This was the paper that printed the article I want to locate."

The brick building had obviously been around for awhile. Ivy grew up the sides and around the faded sign hanging on the front of the building. Like the bed and breakfast, it was one of few structures without a tile roof.

Inside, a front counter separated the rest of the large main room from the entry area.

A young woman with a mop of curly, strawberry blond hair sat the front desk and glanced up from her computer to ask, "May I help you?"

Tempe opened her purse and took out her wallet. Holding up her identification, she said, "Could you help me find a newspaper article about someone?"

"Sure. Do you know the date of the article?"

"Not exactly. If I gave you the name of the person could you locate all the articles about him?"

"Yes, that's easy enough. I'll take you back to one of the computers and show you how to access the old files." She opened the gate into the office. "Come this way."

She led them past several desks all outfitted with computers and monitors, some occupied, others not. Faces turned, some curious, some not. "Do you mind telling me the name of the person you're interested in?"

"Acton Ainsworth," Tempe said.

An odd expression came over the young woman's face. "What's he done now?"

"It's what he's done in the past that I'm interested in," Tempe said.

"What hasn't he done?" the young woman said under her breath. Pointing to an empty desk in a small alcove, she slid out the chair away from the desk and brought another for Hutch. "My name is Candace Rhodes. I used to work for Mr. Ainsworth. He's not a nice man."

"Were you working for him when he was married?" Tempe asked.

"To that artist lady, the one who was murdered? No. I only worked for him for about two weeks. He accused me of prying into his private papers, which I didn't do. He threatened to fire me, but I didn't give him the chance. I quit." She turned on the computer, typed in a password and opened a program. Once in, she keyed in the name Acton Ainsworth. The long list of titles of articles appeared. "You should be able to find what you want."

Tempe sat down in front of the computer. "Thank you, Candace."

"Are you trying to find out if Ainsworth murdered his wife?" she asked.

"He has an alibi for when she was killed," Tempe said, "but he could still be responsible for her death."

Candace nodded, bouncing her strawberry curls. "He probably paid that disgusting Gerald Finnegan to do it."

"Who is Gerald Finnegan?"

"Ainsworth's right-hand man. He's the one who makes sure people pay their bills when they get behind. He's nothing more than a bully. Ainsworth is friendly with the important and socially elite in Santa Barbara. He has one sort of personality for anyone he thinks will help him, but he's a jerk to anyone he considers beneath him."

"Did you ever hear any rumors about Ainsworth and his wife?"

"I've heard plenty, but I've got to get back to the front desk or I might not keep this job." Candace grinned displaying deep dimples.

"I might have some more questions for you before I leave." Tempe sat in front of the computer and used the mouse to scan down the list of articles until she came to "Local Philanthropist Runs Afoul of the Law."

She clicked on it and the article popped up.

"Santa Barbara philanthropist and business man, Acton Ainsworth, was arrested last night for allegedly physically abusing his wife, artist Vanessa Ainsworth. Mrs. Ainsworth was taken to the hospital to be treated for bruises and minor abrasions." The article went on to tell about Acton Ainsworth's work for the Autistic Children's Foundation and his ownership of a successful chain of furniture stores.

"Read this," Tempe said. "The article downplays the fact that Ainsworth abused his wife and plays up his successes and charity work."

Hutch scooted his chair closer. "It sounds like the reporter didn't want to get on Ainsworth's bad side. Read some more. See what happened to him."

A short article reported that Ainsworth pled guilty and was put on probation and ordered to take anger management classes.

"Oh brother," Tempe said. "He more or less got away with it. Guessing by the date on the article, Vanessa managed to get away from him soon after that and filed for divorce."

"Anything else we should know?" Hutch asked.

She scanned for more. Most of the articles praised Ainsworth for his support for autistic children, telling about his presence at other fund raisers and social affairs. "Oh, here's something. 'Vice-President of Ainsworth Furniture Stores Killed in Freak Accident.' This sounds suspicious. The victim was found in his car in one of the ravines off San Marcos Pass."

"I suppose you think Ainsworth's 'hired bully' ran this guy off the road," Hutch said. "Don't you think if that's what happened the Santa Barbara police would have found some evidence?"

"It just sounds suspicious. What did Candace tell us Ainsworth's hired man's name is?"

"Gerald something."

"That's it. Gerald Finnegan." Tempe shut off the computer. "Let's go, I've got one more question for Candace. I want to know what this Finnegan fellow looks like."

# CHAPTER 29

Tempe and Hutch spent the rest of the afternoon wandering through the quaint shops in downtown Santa Barbara. Though Tempe tried to concentrate on the delightful offerings on display, she couldn't help studying reflections in the windows as they passed, looking for someone following them. She spotted no one.

Over a delicious red-snapper dinner in another beach front restaurant, Tempe said, "After talking to Candace, there's no doubt in my mind that Gerald Finnegan is the man who followed me around in Crescent City." Candace had described Finnegan as about the same height as Tempe, muscular, and balding. She also said he had a flat face, kind of a squished nose, and a florid complexion. Tempe only had an impression of the man, but the description seemed to fit.

"If neither Finnegan nor Ainsworth make another move, your part in this will be over, won't it?" Hutch drank some of his water.

"Yes, but even though not responding would be the most intelligent thing for Ainsworth to do, his paranoid personality probably won't allow that."

"If he makes the smarter choice, we go home tomorrow, don't we? I'm sure our room is rented out to someone else tomorrow night. There isn't anything more to do here, is there?"

"No, there isn't. Let's just enjoy our evening. Look out the window. I'm so glad we've been able to enjoy another sunset

184 • MARILYN MEREDITH

over the ocean."

Hutch reached over and grasped Tempe's hand. "I'm sure you're disappointed that Ainsworth didn't confess to his part in his wife's murder."

"I didn't really think it would be that easy. Like Morrison, I hoped by nosing around in Ainsworth's territory I might shake him up enough to do something foolish."

"No matter how this turns out, Ainsworth will be punished. Maybe not the way the detectives and you would like to see, but God knows what he did."

"I know, but that isn't enough for me, and it obviously isn't enough for Vanessa or she wouldn't keep popping up." Tempe ate the last bite of her fish. "Sweetheart, we can't let our guard down until we leave Santa Barbara. We still have one night here."

"I doubt Ainsworth is going to try anything. We don't even know for sure whether or not the SUV that almost ran us down was on purpose or merely an accident."

"No, we don't." No matter how optimistic Hutch might be, Tempe had a deep foreboding that it wasn't over. She felt sure Ainsworth's paranoia wouldn't let him leave them alone.

∽≈

The sun disappeared and fog swirled in again, and along with it the salty scent of the ocean. By the time they reached the parking lot of the bed and breakfast, visibility was down to about a mile.

"Reminds me of home," Hutch said, parking his truck.

"Except it's the wrong time of year for our Tule fog," Tempe said. Fog in the Central Valley settled in right after the first rain, usually the end of November. Only a rainstorm chased it away. Once the rain was over, the fog quickly made its return. "Don't tell me you're getting homesick."

"Not homesick, but I'm ready to head back."

"Me too. This experiment hasn't worked out the way Detective Morrison hoped." Tempe opened her door the same time as Hutch and they both climbed out.

Coming around the back of the truck, Hutch put his arm around Tempe's waist. "This is our last night here, let's make the most of it."

The fog thickened even more. The bed-and-breakfast, with its many turrets and gingerbread trimming, loomed through the gray mist like a haunted house from a movie.

Inside, the effect was not dispelled. The few lights that were on did not reach into all the dark corners. The dining room was totally dark and the parlor so dimly lit, the old-fashioned furniture seemed ominous.

Tempe shivered.

"Are you cold?" Hutch asked, as they started up the staircase to their room.

"No, my grandmother would have said that someone just walked over my grave."

"That's an odd statement."

"Yes, but I'm feeling odd at the moment."

Their room was at one end of the hall. Before they reached it, Dr. Bucklin opened the door to his room and poked his round head out. "Oh, there you are. I'm glad I caught you."

Hutch and Tempe paused and smiled at the portly doctor. He seemed a bit distressed.

"A man came looking for you. When he learned that you were out, he asked if he could slip a note under your door. Denise pointed out your room. There was something about him that I didn't like, so I kept an eye on him. He did go to your room, but he didn't leave a note. All he did was stand there for a moment and stare up and down the hall. My wife says I'm entirely too nosy, but I just had this feeling that he was up to no good. Instead of going back down the way he came, he went to the exit at the other end of the hall and took the back stairs."

"Could you describe this person?" Tempe asked.

"Oh yes. He was Caucasian, wore a baseball cap so I couldn't really see his face. He was about as tall as your husband," he motioned to Tempe, "He wore a leather jacket, but he seemed to have a sturdy build."

"Thank you, that's helpful," Tempe said, glancing at Hutch.

"Is he someone you know?" the doctor asked.

"Someone we're acquainted with. I appreciate you letting us know about him."

"He was up to some sort of mischief, wasn't he?" Dr. Bucklin asked.

"Possibly," Tempe said.

Hutch unlocked the door to their room.

"Um hum, I knew it."

Mrs. Bucklin appeared behind the doctor, her multitude of wrinkles lifted by a smile. "You'll have to excuse my husband. Since his retirement he's taken up reading mystery novels and sees a villain lurking in every corner."

"In this case, he may be right." Tempe smiled at both of their neighbors before following Hutch into their room.

When he'd closed the door and locked it, Hutch asked, "What do you think that means?"

"It means our mysterious man came to call. However, I'm sure he knew we weren't here, he was just checking the layout of the place. I suspect he'll be back."

"What do you want to do?"

Tempe shrugged. "There isn't anything we can do until something happens. I think I better get my gun out of the truck."

"I'll do it."

Tempe would have preferred going herself, but Hutch had already started for the door. "I'll be back in a jiffy," he said.

Sitting on the bed, Tempe thought about what they'd learned. Obviously Gerald Finnegan did Acton Ainsworth's dirty work. He seemed to be an expert at what he did since no one had caught him. Suspecting what Finnegan did for Ainsworth didn't prove anything. If either Finnegan or Ainsworth had any sense, they'd forget about Tempe, and Vanessa Ainsworth's murder would remain unsolved. Ainsworth's paranoia was his biggest enemy. Since Finnegan had been lurking around the bed-and-breakfast, no doubt he and his boss had another devious plan.

Tempe glanced at her watch. Where was Hutch? He seemed to be taking a long time. Stepping to the window, she pulled aside the old fashioned velvet drape and peered down at the parking lot.

Her heart skipped a beat. Despite the thickness of the fog, she could see Hutch's truck. Parked next to it was a dark SUV. She was unable to see Hutch or anyone else. *Oh, my God, please don't let anything happen to Hutch.*

Darting for the door, she grabbed her jacket and purse off the bed. She didn't bother locking the door. Stepping into the hall, she banged on the door opposite theirs.

Without waiting for anyone to answer, she shouted, "Dr. Bucklin, call 911. Tell them there's a problem in the parking lot of the Gingerbread Inn!"

# CHAPTER 30

Hutch removed Tempe's revolver from the glove compartment and stuck it into the pocket of his jacket. He closed the truck door, but before locking it, he noticed the black Suburban parked a couple of spots away. "Oh, oh."

There didn't seem to be anyone inside, nor was there any way to know whether or not it was the same Suburban that had been tailing them. Before moving toward the vehicle, Hutch peered around to see if anyone was lurking about, though it wasn't easy to see anything in the enveloping fog. Most of the people who were staying in the Gingerbread House had probably gone out for the evening. Hutch had no idea what kind of car the doctor and his wife drove—or any of the other people who were staying in the bed and breakfast, for that matter. Maybe the black Suburban belonged to the Bucklins, but the new white Mercedes parked across the way seemed more likely to be theirs.

Hutch wasn't sure what he should do. No doubt Tempe would scout around to see if she could spot someone lurking about. Making a tentative move toward the Suburban, he decided to make sure no one was inside. He squinted through the darkened passenger window of the big SUV, but saw no one, nor was there anything on the black leather seats or the floor to give him a clue as to the owner.

He scratched his head and sighed. Perhaps whoever it was had gone around to the front of the bed-and-breakfast. Feeling silly, pretending to be someone he wasn't, Hutch kept to the shadows and moved slowly. If someone was in hiding, he didn't want to alert him. He couldn't see more than a few yards through the fog, but that was good because it meant no one could see him any better.

Instead of walking on the brick path that led through the garden toward the front of the structure, Hutch decided it would make better sense to go around the other way, through the bushes and plants on the opposite side of the building. That seemed the more likely path of someone up to no good.

It wasn't a good choice. He had to push his way through the enormous elephant leaves and squeeze through thick bamboo. It was like traversing a jungle. But, he reasoned, if a person didn't want to be seen approaching the Gingerbread House, this was the logical way to get there.

A thought struck him that almost made him shudder. What if he did bump into this mysterious Gerald Finnegan? What would he do? Point Tempe's gun at him? And what if the man charged Hutch? Could he possible shoot the man? Hutch knew the answer was no. This entire exercise was stupid.

The best thing for him to do was go upstairs, give Tempe her gun and tell her what he'd found. Nothing.

He shoved his way through giant fern fronds and found himself on the sidewalk in front of the entryway to the inn. Dashing up the front steps, he stopped abruptly when he heard something.

The roar of an engine, followed by what sounded disturbingly like his own truck being started. "Oh, dear God, don't let it be."

He leapt down the stairs and dashed back around the house, the easy way this time. He headed toward the parking lot, arriving in time to see his truck speeding out of the lot. "Tempe," he shouted, knowing that she couldn't possibly hear him.

The Suburban was gone too. His stomach wrenched and he tasted bile.

≈≈

Tempe raced to the fire exit, the one Dr. Bucklin had pointed out earlier as the way Gerald Finnegan had left after checking out her and Hutch's room. Though she'd done nothing more than glance toward the exit when they'd first been shown to their quarters, she'd noticed the steep and uninviting wooden staircase that went down the rear of the building.

The sign on the door read, "Emergency Exit Only, Door Kept Locked." No doubt Finnegan had rigged the door so it could be opened from the outside. Tempe grabbed the handle and flung the door open and peered down the stairs.

She was just in time to see a dark figure clamoring down ahead of her. Finnegan. "Hey, wait up," she hollered.

The man quickened his pace, leaping down the last few steps.

Keeping her hand on the wooden rail, Tempe raced down the stairs after him. Before she reached the bottom, she heard a car start. Peering through the fog, she spotted the black Suburban's back-up lights as it came out of the parking space next to Hutch's truck. With tires screeching, the SUV sped out of the parking lot.

Still running, Tempe opened her purse and rummaged through it until she found her key to the truck. When she reached the driver's door, surprisingly she found it unlocked. She jumped in, pulled the door shut, and started the truck. Jamming the gearshift into reverse, she backed out, and followed the receding red tail lights of the SUV.

The vehicle was almost swallowed by the fog when Tempe drove onto the street.

Stepping on the gas, she sped up until she had the lights in sight again.

Driving so fast through streets she wasn't familiar with in such thick fog was frightening, but not nearly as frightening as wondering what had happened to Hutch. Visions of him lying wounded and bleeding somewhere in the parking lot plagued her. Hopefully, emergency vehicles would arrive quickly and take care of her husband.

Right now she needed to concentrate on staying behind

the black Suburban. Ahead, it sailed through an intersection. She approached the crossroads and couldn't tell the light was red until she'd already entered. No didn't see headlights of approaching cars on either of the side streets, so she didn't pause.

In the distance she heard approaching sirens. She hoped they were headed toward the bed-and-breakfast and not after her.

The dense fog removed Tempe's sense of what little she'd learned about the layout of Santa Barbara's streets. She had no idea where she was driving. All she could do was concentrate of keeping up with the Suburban ahead of her, turning when it turned, and avoiding other vehicles on the road.

Tempe wondered where the mad driver was headed, but when she realized they were beginning to climb, she guessed the destination might be Ainsworth's home. If she had any sense, she'd find a place to turn around and head back to the bed-and-breakfast. But if she did that, her trips to Crescent City and now Santa Barbara would be for nothing. What if Hutch was in the Suburban? Finnegan might have hit him over the head and dumped him in his vehicle. Or something worse.

The fog began to thin and grow wispy. The Suburban sped up and pulled away from Tempe. She stepped on the gas. Amazingly, the fog disappeared completely. As she guessed, they were traveling on San Marcos Pass Road. On her first trip, she'd mainly been interested in the scenery and trying to find the turn off that led to Ainsworth's residence. This time she noticed the metal guardrails lining the edges of black ravines.

The Suburban's tail lights grew smaller and smaller. Tempe pressed the gas pedal trying to catch up. Since she couldn't see lights from any oncoming traffic, she turned on the high beams.

The Suburban disappeared around a sharp curve.

Hoping she'd spot the back of the vehicle as soon as she'd reached the same curve, Tempe concentrated on the highway.

Without warning, painfully bright headlights came right

at her. She switched her own lights to low beam, but the lights hurtled onward. She squinted. It was the black Suburban. It was in her lane.

She swerved to the left. The SUV came at her, banging into the right fender. Even though she slammed on the brakes, the truck veered across the other lane, slamming against the guardrail on the left hand side of the road.

The Suburban backed up. The engine revved. It came at her again, striking the side of the truck full force. The truck was jammed against the guardrail again. The sound of wrenched metal grated in Tempe's ears. She could feel the truck losing traction on the asphalt. The guardrail gave way and the truck leaned sideways.

Tempe prayed as she'd never prayed before. If she went over the edge in the truck, no one would ever know where to look for her.

Once again the Suburban ran full throttle into the side of the truck. The airbag exploded. It struck Tempe's face and chest, knocking the breath out of her. She felt pain, as though her nose might be broken, and her knuckles ached. But that was the least of her problems.

For one long moment, the truck teetered back and forth. The Suburban backed away again. Tempe knew that her vehicle was going over the side and she could do nothing about it.

All at once, the truck tipped over and slid on the driver's side down a steep incline. Tempe's heart banged in her chest. The truck slipped roughly, bumping against rocks and other obstructions, shuddering, then moving again. Scraping and sliding. *Wasn't it ever coming to a stop?*

# CHAPTER 31

The siren announced the approach of a Santa Barbara police car. Flashing emergency lights were visible before the black-and-white unit. Hutch stood on the front porch of the Gingerbread House waving his arms as the police car braked to a stop.

Two uniformed officers stepped out. A thick-chested middle-aged policeman frowned at Hutch. "What seems to be the trouble, sir?"

How could he explain such a complicated scenario? "My wife is missing and I think she's in terrible danger. We've got to go after her."

"Let's start in the beginning. Who are you and who is your wife?" the older policeman asked.

Hutch took a deep breath in an attempt to calm himself. "I'm Pastor Hutch Hutchinson. My wife, Tempe Crabtree, is a deputy sheriff from Tulare County."

The driver, taller and thinner, joined his partner at the bottom of the steps. "What makes you think something has happened to her?"

The front door burst open and Dr. and Mrs. Bucklin popped out. Obviously out of breath, the doctor joined Hutch. "Oh, thank goodness, the police are here. I called 911 as soon as your wife told me."

The muscular officer stared at Dr. Bucklin. "Where did you see her?"

Before he could answer, Denise, the owner of the bed

and breakfast stepped outside, wrapping a sweater around her. "What's going on?"

"That's what we're trying to find out," the first officer said, staring pointedly at Hutch.

"Please," Hutch read the man's name from his metal name tag, "Officer Zebroski. It's complicated. My wife is investigating a man named Acton Ainsworth."

The two police officers exchanged glances.

"We've been followed around and nearly run over by one of his employees…"

Officer Zebroski interrupted, "Gerald Finnegan."

"Yes, we believe that is the man. Anyway, I think my wife is chasing him in my truck. Finnegan was here tonight."

Dr. Bucklin eagerly added, "Yes, I saw him. He was snooping around the Hutchinsons' room earlier."

The other officer reached out his hand and shook Hutch's. "I'm Officer Frazier. I think you should come with us to the station and tell your story to our sergeant."

"No, we need to find Tempe right now. I know she's in trouble."

Zebroski opened the back door. "Sir, get in the car. We need to go to the station first."

"Is there something we can do?" Dr. Bucklin asked.

"Someone should have let me know there was a problem," Denise said.

Before Hutch slid into the backseat, he said, "If Tempe should call or turn up, please call the police station."

As the police car drove through the city streets, siren blaring, lights flashing, Hutch made another attempt to explain what was going on. "Acton Ainsworth's wife was murdered in Bear Creek where we live."

"Yeah, I heard about that," Zebroski said.

"My wife and her superiors believe Mr. Ainsworth is responsible for her death."

"I thought he had an alibi."

"Yes, he does, but he still may be the one responsible."

"You're thinking he hired that thug Finnegan to kill her,"

Frazier said, matter-of-factly. At the same time Zebroski used the car radio to communicate with the police station.

Hutch prayed silently not only for Tempe's safety but his own as the police car careened around vehicles that barely had time to get out of the way. The fog was so thick, Hutch wondered how the officers could see where they were going.

A sprawling two-story white stucco building loomed out of the mist. No doubt it had a red tile roof like nearly all the buildings in Santa Barbara, but it was impossible to tell because of the low fog. The police unit screeched to a stop at the curb near the front entrance. "Let's hurry," Zebroski said when he opened the back door for Hutch.

Together, they rushed up the steps to the front door accented by a high arch. Inside, Hutch was quickly ushered into to a medium sized office. After quick introductions, the sergeant, a gray-haired stocky Hispanic, Sergeant Lopez, said, "I think I've got the basic idea of what's going on. I tried to find out something from the Tulare County Sheriff's Department concerning this case, but no one seems to know anything."

Hutch put his hands on Lopez's desk and leaned toward him. "That's because when my wife was asked to come here and find out what she could about Acton Ainsworth, they told her that if she got in trouble she was on her own. They said they wouldn't even acknowledge that they sent her."

Sergeant Lopez compressed his lips and stared at Hutch. "And she's in trouble?"

"Yes, sir, I think she is."

"Do you have any idea where she might be?"

"She took off after the black Suburban in my truck. Maybe you've had some reports of a vehicle like that and a white truck racing through town."

"As a matter of fact we have, but we've been tied up with fog-related traffic accidents. Last reports were that they were headed toward the San Marcos Pass Road."

Frantic, Hutch ran his fingers through his already rumpled hair. "We have to go after them." He patted his pocket. "I have her gun here, but she thinks it's in the glove compartment of the truck."

"Okay. Zebroski, Frazier, take the preacher here and see if you can catch up with his wife."

Relieved and anxious, Hutch was the first one out the door.

※ ※

The truck quit sliding. It shuddered, and slowly flipped over on its top.

An odd thought popped into Tempe's head. *Hutch's poor truck. It'll never be the same.* Then she giggled. Here she was hanging upside down, suspended by the seat belt harness, her nose dripping blood, being pursued by a murderer and she was worried about her husband's new truck. Not badly injured, she knew it was time to get out of the vehicle, see where she was and how hard it was going to be to get back up to the highway and signal someone.

Struggling, she finally managed to unhook the seat belt, landing heavily on her shoulder and back against the roof of the car. Surprisingly, the engine was still running. She turned off the ignition.

*Get out of the truck.*

That wasn't going to be easy. The driver's side door was dented. As was the passenger door and it seemed to be worse. Shoving hard while working the handle, she managed to move the driver's door open a bit. Bracing her feet on the door, she shoved with all her strength. It only budged a few more inches. She did it again and it creaked open a bit.

Just maybe she could squeeze through the opening. As she maneuvered her body around and put her head through, she heard something that chilled her heart.

A shower of rocks and dirt struck the car. Someone was making his way down the cliff.

She heard the unmistakable sound of shoes or boots sometimes sliding on the loose gravel. The beam of a flashlight jerked and flickered. Though it might be someone coming to rescue her, in her heart she knew it was the driver of the Suburban who wanted to make sure she hadn't survived the crash. As much as she'd been curious about Gerald Finnegan, she had no desire to face him now.

Pulling back, she quickly pulled the keys from the ignition, reached up to unlock the glove compartment. It opened easily, but when she felt around inside there was nothing there but papers. No gun. Hutch must have retrieved it before he'd disappeared. Was he dead? *Oh, God, please no.*

The sounds of the person coming down the steep slope grew louder. She wouldn't have a chance if she remained in the truck. She wouldn't have much even if she did make it out—but at least she'd have some kind of a chance.

Wriggling and shoving with all her strength against the door, Tempe managed to squeeze through the narrow opening. She squatted beside the upside down vehicle, surveying the scene. The truck was balanced precariously on the edge of a cliff. It had come to rest against a giant oak tree. Peering up the hill, she could see the flashlight beam bobbing as the dark figure behind it moved jerkily toward her.

Reaching around her on the ground, Tempe found a good-sized rock and grasped it in her hand. Not much of a weapon, but better than nothing.

In the distance, a siren whined. Was someone coming to investigate the hole in the railing? Perhaps Dr. Bucklin had explained enough to the police that they were actually searching for her. Maybe, the police had found Hutch and he was able to tell them what had been going on. If so, that meant Hutch was alive. Was that too much to hope for?

# CHAPTER 32

Hutch hadn't completely fastened his seat belt when Officer Frazier started the police car, revved the engine and made a quick U-turn.

"Hang on," Zebroski warned a bit too late.

Hutch pitched forward in the back seat.

At least they weren't wasting any time. The siren and emergency lights were on as they sped through the thick fog toward the turnoff to the Marcos Pass Highway. Hutch was glad the police officers were familiar with the streets. From his vantage point all he could see was the swirling mist.

Once he could tell they were climbing, the fog began to thin, and then almost miraculously, disappeared completely.

"Can you see my truck or the black Suburban up ahead?" Hutch asked.

"Not yet," Zebroski said.

They sped on in silence, the only sounds coming from the police radio—static and voices speaking with code numbers. None of it made sense to Hutch. A couple of times, Zebroski picked up the mike and responded.

"Hey," Frazier said. "Up ahead there's a black Suburban parked the wrong way on the side of the road."

"Oh, oh, looks like there's been an accident. I'll call it in."

Hutch could see the black Suburban parked at an odd angle and a break in the barrier. "Oh, dear God, let Tempe be okay."

Traffic slowed to get around the Suburban. Frazier stopped the police unit nosing the front end against the Suburban's grill.

"Maybe you better stay in the car, Preacher," Zebroski said.

"Not on your life," Hutch announced. "Let me out. I promise not to get in the way."

Reluctantly, Zebroski opened the passenger door.

Hutch climbed out. The first thing he noticed was the big dent in the Suburban's grill. The second thing he noticed was white paint on the crinkled fender. "Oh, my God! Where is Tempe?" He ran to the edge of the cliff, but it was too dark to see anything.

"I'm calling for back-up and an ambulance," Frazier said.

⚜

Tempe crouched behind the slightly open door of the truck. The approaching footsteps grew louder.

Her pursuer slipped and another shower of stones rained down on the truck. "Damn."

The voice sounded familiar. Had she ever heard Gerald Finnegan speak? She didn't think so.

Gripping the rock in her fist, Tempe waited.

When he was close enough, she heard his ragged breathing from the exertion of making his way down the hill. She stood. She was as shocked as the man who stood in front of her. Obviously, he expected or hoped that she had been killed or badly injured.

Instead of Gerald Finnegan, it was Acton Ainsworth. His eyes were big. His right hand held a gun. "I am sick and tired of you. You've driven me crazy. Everything was perfect until you started poking around."

"I didn't expect to see you. I figured you gave your handyman orders to take care of me just like you had him kill Vanessa."

"We underestimated you. Finnegan and I were convinced that finding that pig's heart on your doorstep would discourage you from messing in my business."

"Actually, if you'd not done anything I wouldn't be here now."

He didn't seem to hear her. "Finnegan screwed up his dealings with you," Ainsworth said. "I realized I wasn't going to have any peace until you were out of my life. Obviously I have to take care of you myself." He raised the gun.

At the same time the siren grew louder. Tempe noticed the emergency lights flashing high above them. "You can't shoot me now. The police are here and they'll know it isn't an accident."

Ainsworth growled, "Then I'll have to make sure you go the rest of the way down the cliff." He lunged toward Tempe, one hand outstretched.

She side-stepped his charge, aimed the rock and bashed it against Ainsworth's forehead.

He groaned and stumbled. "You're going to pay for this." He staggered toward her, but it was obvious he'd been surprised by the blow.

Tempe hit him again and he fell to his knees. He dropped the gun. Tempe scooped it up and pointed it at him.

A lump rose on his forehead. He appeared stunned, as though he couldn't believe what was happening.

"Tempe, are you okay?" Hutch called from above.

Someone else hollered, "Deputy Crabtree, we're coming down."

"I'm fine, but Acton Ainsworth isn't," she called back. "Don't move, Mr. Ainsworth, or I'll have to shoot."

The sound of people slipping and sliding down the hill drew Ainsworth's attention. "You can't do this to me. I'm a very important man around here. No one will believe anything you tell them."

"That may have worked in the past, Mr. Ainsworth, but it isn't going to work now."

"I didn't do anything," he whined.

"You tried to kill me just like you killed your wife."

"I didn't kill my wife," he sputtered.

"You got Gerald Finnegan to do it for you," Tempe said. She glanced up and saw one uniformed officer had almost reached them. Hutch and another officer followed.

Hutch hollered, "Be careful, Tempe, we're coming."

Focused on Tempe, Ainsworth didn't seem to notice. "Vanessa deserved to die. When she divorced me she tried to ruin my reputation by accusing me of all sorts of horrible things. The judge rewarded her with a huge settlement and monthly alimony she didn't deserve."

A bulky police officer reached them first. His name tag identified him as

Officer Zebroski. Expressionless, he stepped closer to Ainsworth. "Put your hands behind your back Mr. Ainsworth, you're under arrest."

Ainsworth displayed his teeth in an ugly smile at Zebroski. "You've got this all wrong, Officer. This woman attacked me. Look at this knot on my head."

The second police officer patted Ainsworth down before pulling his arms behind his back and cuffed him.

Zebroski began, "You have the right to remain silent…."

The entire time Zebroski read Ainsworth's his rights, he glared at Tempe. When Zebroski finished he asked Ainsworth, "Do you understand?"

"Yes, I understand." To Tempe, Ainsworth added, "This is all your fault. If you hadn't been poking around in affairs that had nothing to do with you, none of this would have happened."

"It had plenty to do with me. Your wife was murdered in my territory," Tempe said.

"I'll take the gun now, Deputy," Zebroski held out his hand toward her.

Tempe put the revolver in his palm. "This belongs to Ainsworth. He planned to shoot me with it."

"Your aren't listening to me. She attacked me with a rock," Ainsworth whined. "I probably have a concussion. I need to see a doctor."

"You'll be taken care of," Frazier said. "An ambulance is

on the way. Get going up that hill." The police officers each grabbed of one of Ainsworth's elbows and began pulling and pushing him up the steep hill.

Hutch embraced Tempe. "Are you all right? You have blood all over your face."

"That's from my nose. I'm sore but nothing seems to be broken. I'm afraid your beautiful new truck is though."

"Don't worry, my insurance is paid. I bet Ainsworth's is too."

≈≈

The climb back up the ravine was a lot more difficult and took much longer than the slide down in the truck. Tempe was glad for Hutch's help.

When they finally reached the top, an ambulance was parked behind the patrol car. Acton Ainsworth continued to protest his innocence and holler about Tempe's brutality as Zebroski helped him into the back of the ambulance. The officer climbed in behind him. Once the doors were shut, the ambulance took off.

A tow truck was sent for the Suburban and arrangements were made for another to pull Hutch's truck out of the ravine. Though Hutch and the police officers wanted Tempe to be checked by a doctor, she refused. "I'm okay, only banged up a bit." Hutch's handkerchief was used to wipe the blood off her face. They rode back to the police station with Frazier.

Sergeant Lopez had called in his Deputy Chief, no doubt after he'd learned that Acton Ainsworth had tried to kill a deputy from Tulare County. Nearly two hours were spent relating everything that had happened, beginning with Vanessa Ainsworth's body being found in the aftermath of the forest fire, Tempe's trip to Crescent City, the pig's heart left on the doorstep of her home, and what had happened after they arrived in Santa Barbara. Everything said was recorded on tape. Hutch filled in what Tempe forgot.

After she told the Deputy Chief and Sergeant Lopez about going to Ainsworth's Fine Furniture store to make an appointment with Acton Ainsworth, the Deputy Chief asked, "Why did you do that?"

Tempe explained all that had led up to Detective Morrison and Sergeant Guthrie asking her to see what she could find out by confronting Ainsworth. She ended with, "It wasn't an assignment sanctioned by the department. It's just that the investigation into Vanessa Ainsworth's murder had reached a dead end, even though everyone suspected that Ainsworth was responsible. When that pig's heart was left on my front step, the case became personal."

"Did this detective and sergeant realize how dangerous sending you here to bait Ainsworth would be?" Lopez asked.

Tempe nodded. "That's the only reason they allowed my husband to come with me."

Lopez glanced at Hutch. Though he didn't say anything it was obvious he didn't think Hutch had been much protection. "So then what happened?"

When Tempe reached the part where they thought Gerald Finnegan had visited the bed and breakfast, she said, "We were wrong about that. If we'd paid more attention to Dr. Bucklin's description we might have guessed it was Ainsworth, not Finnegan."

"Why? What did the doctor say?" Lopez asked.

"Though Ainsworth was wearing the same kind of clothes as Finnegan, the doctor told us the man at our door was my husband's height. I knew Finnegan was only tall as me."

Tempe finished with only a few interruptions from Sgt. Lopez and the Deputy Chief. Tempe and Hutch signed papers that stated everything they'd said was the truth.

"How long are you planning to stay in Santa Barbara?" the Deputy Chief asked.

Tempe and Hutch looked at each other. Tempe said, "We plan to leave in the morning."

"Leave a phone number where you can be reached. We may have more questions for you. I'm sure you're aware that you'll be expected to testify when this comes to trial."

⁂

When they finally stepped inside their room in the Gingerbread Inn, Hutch took Tempe in his arms. "I have something to say to you."

Every bone in Tempe's body ached, and her eyes felt like they were filled with sand. "Can't it wait, sweetheart? I am so tired I can hardly think."

"No, I have to say this right now." He smoothed away the hair that had come loose from her braid and fell across her forehead. "I'm so sorry."

"Sorry? For what?"

"It's my fault that you didn't have your gun with you. I almost lost you because of how I feel about you carrying a gun. You have no idea how frightened I was. If that crazy man had killed you, I'd never have forgiven myself. I'll never ever say anything about your gun again."

"You don't have to take all the blame. I should have remembered the gun was in the glove compartment and taken it upstairs with me when we got home." Though Hutch's apology was nice and it would be great not to have him complain about her carrying when she wasn't on duty, all she could really think about was climbing into bed.

He pulled her against him and hugged her tightly. "I love you so much."

"I know you do and I love you too, but please, I need to go to sleep."

He nodded and released her.

☙❧

Before they could make arrangements to leave in the morning, they were surrounded by the other guests of the bed and breakfast as well as Denise, the owner. The thin woman held out the local newspaper and displayed the front page. The head line read, "Local Business Man Arrested for Attempted Murder."

Denise stood with her arms crossed. "You're not leaving until you fill us in."

"I called 911 like you told me to," Dr. Bucklin interjected, a huge grin on his face.

"Thank you for that," Hutch said.

"And thank you for being so observant," Tempe added.

"Is it true that Acton Ainsworth tried to kill you?" Dr. Bucklin asked.

Tempe nodded. "Yes, it is." She glanced at Hutch. "I suppose you might as well know the rest. I came here to find out if Mr. Ainsworth had anything to do with his wife's death, even though he had an alibi for the time it happened. He actually confessed to me that he hired someone to kill his wife. I'm sure they'll have more details in the next edition of the paper."

"Ainsworth wrecked my truck and we need transportation to get home. Could someone take us to a rental car agency?"

Immediately, Dr. Bucklin volunteered, no doubt hoping for more information about the real-life mystery.

∽≈

Arriving back in Dennison, before driving all the way to Bear Creek, Hutch parked the compact rental sedan in front of the sheriff's sub-station in Dennison.

"Seems like this could wait," Hutch said.

"I know, but this is what Sergeant Guthrie told me to do." She noticed the detective's black Mercury SUV parked several vehicles away. "Looks like Morrison is here too."

Not only Detective Morrison and Sergeant Guthrie awaited Tempe, but Richards was there too. Surprisingly, all three stood when they saw Tempe. Even more shocking were the big grins they displayed.

Tempe glanced back at Hutch, who beamed back at the other three men.

Morrison reached out and grabbed Tempe's hand in his big fist. "Congratulations, Crabtree. You did it."

"Good job," Richards said.

Sergeant Guthrie motioned them inside. "Both of you, take a seat."

All four of them crowded around Guthrie's desk. There was barely room for the two big men, Tempe and Hutch. "We have some news for you, Crabtree," Sgt. Guthrie said. "Morrison, do you want to tell her?"

Tempe couldn't get over how a smile changed the countenance of the usually ferocious looking detective.

Sitting next to her, Morrison said, "When the Santa Barbara police went up to Ainsworth's home this morning looking for his hit man, Gerald Finnegan, they found him all right. Deader'n a door nail. Bullet hole through his forehead. Shot with Ainsworth's gun. The same one that he threatened you with. Ainsworth isn't getting out of this one. You did good, Crabtree."

Richards leaned forward so Tempe could see his face. When he smiled, his narrow eyes lit up, and all the lines that usually made him look like he was squinting, lifted into a grin. "When Morrison told me his crazy idea, I was dead set against it, but he was right. If you hadn't gone over there, we'd have never solved Vanessa Ainsworth's murder."

"I couldn't have done it without Hutch." Tempe squeezed her husband's hand.

Guthrie rose from behind his desk and shook Hutch's hand. "Thanks, Pastor Hutchinson."

"Am I going to get any time off?" Tempe asked.

"Heck no," Guthrie snapped, but his eyes sparkled with merriment. "How many vacations do you need?"

≈≈

Guthrie gave her the rest of the day off, with her regular schedule beginning again on Friday night.

Since Vanessa had not visited during their last night at the bed-and-breakfast, Tempe felt sure that the murdered woman's spirit was finally at rest.

Back at home, Tempe called Abigail Jacoby and let her know what had transpired with Acton Ainsworth.

"Thank you, Tempe," Abby said. "Come back and visit one of these days. You're always welcome."

When Tempe hung up the phone, she turned to Hutch. "There were times I wasn't sure our trip to Santa Barbara was going to have the desired results, but together we forced Acton Ainsworth to reveal what he'd done."

Hutch put his arms around Tempe and pulled her close. "I'm just happy you're safe. I was terrified when you took off in my truck and I knew you didn't have your gun. I promise I'll never ask you to lock up your gun again."

"I thought you had been injured or worse, maybe even kidnapped, that's why I took off after the Suburban." She was quiet for a moment before adding, "I'm so sorry about your new truck."

"It can be replaced." He cupped the back of her head and pressed his lips to her forehead. She reveled in his scent, his warmth, and the knowledge of his feelings. The best thing that had happened was the tension between them had disappeared. "I love you, Hutch."

"And I love you, Tempe."

*The End*

# More About The Near Extermination of the Tolowa

In 1851, California Governor, Pete Burnett stated, "…that a war of extermination will continue to be waged between two races until the Indian race becomes extinct, must be expected. While we cannot anticipate the result with but painful regret, the inevitable destiny of the race is beyond the power and wisdom of man to avert."

Miners, settlers and other whites treated anyone of native ancestry as slightly less than human. "Volunteer armies" of white men invaded peaceful Indian villages and killed everyone in sight, men, women and children.

In 1853, in the Tolowa village of Yontoket, nearly 500 people gathered to pray and worship, thanking God for life. Dressed like soldiers, a group of citizens from Crescent City formed a "volunteer army." They attacked the worshipping Indians, firing on anyone who moved. More than 450 Tolowa were murdered that night. The whites built a huge fire and burned all the sacred ceremonial clothing, the regalia and feathers. They tossed the babies into the flames, some of them still alive. Weights were tied around the necks of the dead and they were thrown into the nearby water.

Some Tolowa escaped the massacre and fled to the mountains. Two men who had been in the sacred sweathouse crept away and hid under the water, using reeds to breathe. The next morning, the water was red with the blood of their people.

The following year, a party of white men armed with guns, hid in the brush around a Tolowa village. When the Indians stepped out of their homes, they were slaughtered. The few who managed to survive ran to Lake Earl and jumped into the water. The white men followed. Whenever a head popped out of the water, the men shot at it.

"We hope that the government will render such aid as will enable the citizens of the north to carry on a war of extermination until the last redskin of these tribes has been killed. Extermination is no longer a question of time—the time has arrived, the work has commenced, and let the first man that says treaty or peace be regarded as a traitor."—The Yreka Herald, 1853.

Smith River Rancheria was established by the federal government in the mid 1800s. In 1868 it was annulled. Years later, allotments were granted to separate Tolowa families through the Smith River basin area and eventually a rancheria was established.

In 1960, President Dwight Eisenhower terminated both the Smith River and Elk Valley Rancherias and the Tolowa were told they were not a recognized tribe.

In 1983, the Tolowa regained recognition as a tribe and the rancherias were re-established.

There are some who still want the Tolowa to be recognized as a nation.

# ABOUT THE AUTHOR

Marilyn Meredith is the author of over twenty books in several genres, but mainly mystery. She embraced electronic publishing before anyone knew much about it.

She teaches writing and was an instructor for Writer's Digest School, has been a judge for several writing contest, was a founding member of the San Joaquin chapter of Sisters in Crime, serves on the board of directors of the Public Safety Writers Association, is also a member of EPIC and Mystery Writers of America.

Marilyn lives in the foothills of the Southern Sierra in California in a place much like Bear Creek where her heroine Tempe Crabtree serves as a resident deputy. She is married to the "cute sailor" she met on a blind date many years ago and is grateful for all the support he gives her and her writing career every day.

She is proud of the fact that she and her husband raised five children and now are grandparents to nineteen and great-grands to eleven.